Casey Had A Way Of Getting To Him Like No Other Woman Ever Had.

Not something Jackson wanted to admit even to himself, let alone her. But it was there. A niggling tug of desire that was damned hard to ignore. He stopped alongside her table, opened his mouth to speak and then slammed it shut again.

Beside her on the red vinyl booth was a child's booster seat. And in that seat was a baby girl. Jackson scowled as the infant—surely not even a year old yet—turned her face up to his and grinned, displaying two tiny white teeth.

And *his* eyes.

Tearing his gaze from the child, Jackson glared at Casey and ground out, "Just what the *hell* is going on?"

Dear Reader,

Do you ever wonder if a decision you make will come back to haunt you? Sure you do. We all do.

In *Falling for King's Fortune,* two people find out just what can happen when Fate steps into their lives.

Casey Davis, alone in the world and craving family, visits a sperm bank, eventually gives birth to her daughter and thinks her world couldn't be better. Then an anonymous source tells her who her child's father is and before she knows it, Casey's life is spinning out of control.

Jackson King is the youngest of the King brothers and the most adventurous. He goes where he wants when he wants and likes his life just as it is. But when everything changes on him, Jackson has to decide if love isn't the *real* adventure.

I hope you enjoyed the KINGS OF CALIFORNIA trilogy as much as I enjoyed writing them. I'm planning on revisiting the Kings, since as it turns out, there are a lot of King cousins yet to be heard from!

Please stop by my Web site at www.maureenchild.com and drop me an e-mail! Or write to me snail mail at P.O. Box 1883, Westminster, CA 92684-1883.

Happy Reading!

Maureen

MAUREEN CHILD

FALLING FOR KING'S FORTUNE

Published by Silhouette Books
America's Publisher of Contemporary Romance

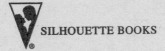 SILHOUETTE BOOKS

ISBN-13: 978-0-373-76868-4
ISBN-10: 0-373-76868-0

FALLING FOR KING'S FORTUNE

Books by Maureen Child

Silhouette Desire

**Expecting Lonergan's Baby #1719
**Strictly Lonergan's Business #1724
**Satisfying Lonergan's Honor #1730
The Part-Time Wife #1755
Beyond the Boardroom #1765
Thirty Day Affair #1785
†Scorned by the Boss #1816
†Seduced by the Rich Man #1820
†Captured by the Billionaire #1826
††Bargaining for King's Baby #1857
††Marrying for King's Millions #1862
††Falling for King's Fortune #1868

Silhouette Nocturne

‡Eternally #4
‡Nevermore #10

**Summer of Secrets
‡The Guardians
†Reasons for Revenge
††Kings of California

MAUREEN CHILD

is a California native who loves to travel. Every chance they get, she and her husband are taking off on another research trip. The author of more than sixty books, Maureen loves a happy ending and still swears that she has the best job in the world. She lives in Southern California with her husband, two children and a golden retriever with delusions of grandeur.

You can contact Maureen via her Web site: www.maureenchild.com.

To Sarah…for too many reasons to list here
I love you

One

"I've been stood up." Jackson King closed his cell phone with a snap. Setting his empty glass down on the lustrously polished bar top, he signaled the bartender, Eddie, an older man with knowing eyes, to fill it again.

"Well," Eddie said, "I think this is a first for you, isn't it? You losing your touch?"

Jackson snorted a laugh and leaned deeper into the cushioned back of the dark red bar stool. Swiveling it a half turn, he glanced over the dimly lit room behind him. The Hotel Franklin, the only five-star hotel between the tiny town of Birkfield and Sacramento, boasted one of the best bars in the state.

It was also conveniently close to the King family airfield where Jackson spent most of his time. He kept a suite in the hotel for those nights when he was too tired to drive home and thought of the elegant bar almost as his office.

"Oh hell no. That's never going to happen. Wasn't a woman who blew me off, Eddie," Jackson said with a grin. "My cousin Nathan canceled on me. His assistant was driving his car to his mountain place and had problems. Nathan to the rescue."

"Ah." The bartender nodded. "Good to know you're not slipping. Thought maybe it was a sign of the apocalypse or something."

He did have good luck with women, Jackson mused. Or at least, he always had. Soon enough, all of that would be over. He frowned a little at the thought.

"Something wrong?" The bartender asked.

Jackson shot him a look. "Nothing I want to talk about."

"Right. Another drink. Coming right up."

While he waited, Jackson let his gaze slide around the elegantly appointed bar. The room gleamed with a warm glow as discreet lighting reflected off the wood walls and marble floors. The mahogany bar itself curved around the room in a sinuous bend that was nearly artistic. Tall, high-backed red leather stools were pulled up to the bar inviting patrons to sit and stay awhile. Small round tables spotted the floor, each of them boasting flickering candlelight. And the soft, lazy strains of jazz piped in through overhead speakers.

In this bar a man could relax and a lone woman could enjoy a quiet drink without being hassled. At the moment, the place was practically empty. There were two couples at the tables and at the far end of the bar, a woman sat alone, like Jackson. Instinctively, Jackson's gaze fixed on the blond woman and he smiled. She gave him a long, sly look that fired his blood before returning her attention to her martini.

"She's a looker all right," Eddie muttered as he refilled Jackson's glass with his favorite, Irish whiskey.

"What?"

"The blonde." The bartender risked a quick look himself. "Saw you spot her. She's been sitting over there for an hour, nursing that one drink and acting like she's waiting for someone."

"Yeah?" Jackson took a longer look. Even from a distance there was something about the woman that made his blood start to hum. He began to think that maybe Nathan not showing up was a very good thing.

"Can't imagine anyone standing *her* up," Eddie said as he moved off to fill another order.

Jackson couldn't either. This was a woman who demanded a man's attention. He watched her long fingers move up and down the stem of her martini glass in slow strokes and his body jerked to attention as strongly as if her hand was moving across his skin.

She looked up and her gaze slammed into his. He couldn't see her eyes from here, but he had a feeling there was a knowing gleam in them. She knew he was watching her. Had probably done the whole stroke-the-crystal thing on purpose to get his attention. Well congratulations, babe, it worked.

Picking up his drink, Jackson casually walked the length of the bar, slipping from lamplight to shadow, his gaze continually fixed on the blonde who watched his approach. As he got closer, he could appreciate the view even more.

She smiled, and a blast of something hot and driving roared up inside him. He hadn't felt anything like that in…well, ever. Instantaneous heat. Even from a distance, she was affecting him in ways he never would have expected. Possibilities opened up in front of him as he closed the distance between them.

She swiveled on the bar stool as he approached and Jackson took that moment to size her up completely. She wasn't very tall, maybe five foot five, but she was wearing sky-high, black-heeled sandals that would give her an extra few inches. Her blond hair was short, cut close to her head, and small gold hoops in her ears twinkled in the light as she tipped her head to look at him. Her sapphire-blue dress had long sleeves, a full, short skirt and a V neck that dipped low enough to showcase breasts that were just the right size.

Her big eyes were blue and focused on him and one corner of her mouth was tipped up in an inviting smile as he stopped beside her.

"This seat taken?"

"It is now," she said and her voice was a whisper that sounded like long nights and lazy mornings.

He shot his cuffs, straightened his dark red tie, slid onto the stool beside hers and said, "I'm Jackson and you're beautiful."

She laughed and shook her head. "Does that line always work?"

He nodded to her in acknowledgement. "More often than not. How's it doing tonight?"

"I'll let you know after you buy me another drink."

Oh yeah. He'd have to remember to thank Nathan for blowing him off tonight. Turning, he signaled Eddie for a refill, then looked back at her. Close up, her eyes were as blue as the deep sapphire of her dress. Her mouth was tinted a deep pink and her lips were lush and full, tempting him to lean in and take what he wanted.

But he could wait. Waiting was half the fun.

"So, do I get to know your name?"

"Casey. You can call me Casey."

"Pretty name."

"Not really," she said, shrugging one shoulder. "My full name is Cassiopeia."

Jackson grinned. "Well, that's prettier."

She returned the smile and Jackson could have sworn he actually *felt* his blood start to simmer. The woman packed a hell of a punch with that smile.

"No, it's really not. Not when you're ten years old and your friends have names like Tiffany or Brittney or Amber…"

"So, you went with the short version."

She glanced up at Eddie with a murmured "thank you," as the bartender delivered her bright green Appletini. "I did," she said. "And have my father to thank for it. My mother loved Greek myths, hence my name. My father loved baseball. Hence the nickname."

Jackson blinked, then laughed, getting the connection instantly. "Casey Stengel?"

Surprise flickered briefly in her eyes. "I'm impressed that you know the name. Most in our generation don't."

Jackson eased into the conversation, realizing he was having a good time. It was more than just her sex appeal, he was enjoying talking to her, too. He couldn't remember the last time that had happened. "Please. You're talking to a man who still has truckloads of his old baseball cards carefully tucked away in storage."

She lifted her drink, put her lips around the straw and sucked. Jackson went hard as stone in an instant. His mouth was dry and his heartbeat thundered in his ears. He wasn't sure if she was deliberately trying to set him on fire, but whether she was or not, the result was the same.

While he watched, she crossed her legs in a slow slide of skin against skin and one sandaled foot began to swing. One of her hands cupped the bowl of her drink glass while the other stroked the stem, as she'd done before.

Now he was sure she was doing it deliberately. Because her dark blue eyes were fixed on his as if she were measuring his reaction. Well, he'd been playing this kind of game for years. She'd see what he wanted her to see and nothing else.

When she set her drink down, she swept her tongue across her top lip as if searching for any errant drops of liquor. Jackson's gaze followed the motion and his insides fisted even tighter. Damn, she was good.

"So, Casey," he asked idly, "what are your plans for the evening?"

"I don't have any," she admitted. "You?"

His gaze dropped from her face to her breasts and back up again. "Nothing special until a few minutes ago. Now, I can think of a few ideas off the top of my head."

She chewed at her bottom lip as if she were suddenly nervous, but he wasn't buying it. Her moves were all too smooth. She was far too sure of herself. She'd set out to seduce him and she was doing a hell of a job of it.

Ordinarily, Jackson preferred to be the one making the moves. But tonight, he was willing to make an exception. Mainly because the deed was done and he wanted her more than he wanted to take another breath. "Why don't you let me buy you dinner at the hotel restaurant? We could get to know each other a little better."

She smiled, but her heart wasn't in it. Glancing around, as if to assure herself the two of them were secluded at the shadowy, far end of the bar, she looked back at him and said, "I'm not really in the mood for dinner, thanks."

"Really?" Intrigued again, he asked, "Then what?"

"Actually, I've wanted to kiss you since the moment I first saw you."

Good. She was going to be as upfront about this as he planned to be. "I'm a big believer in going after what you want."

"I'll bet you are," she murmured.

Her voice sounded breathless and he could feel her tension in the air. A tension he shared. All Jackson could think about was kissing her. Forget dinner. The only taste he wanted in his mouth was *her.*

Oh, he *definitely* owed Nathan.

"The question," Jackson said quietly, his gaze linking with hers, daring her to look away, "is whether or not *you* believe in doing exactly what you want."

"Why don't we find out?" She leaned forward and he met her halfway, more than eager to get a taste of this woman. In mere minutes, she'd driven him to the edge of a raw desire the likes of which he'd never known before.

Their lips met and in that instant, electricity hummed between them. There was no other way to describe it. Jackson felt the burn, the rush, and gave himself up to it. There in the shadows, his mouth moved over hers, his blood practically steaming in his veins.

Her scent—lavender—filled him and clouded his mind. All he could concentrate on was the incredible feel of her mouth on his, even as he told himself to pull back. To not push this too far too fast. This was something he wanted to enjoy. To revel in. And to do that, they'd need somewhere more private than the darkened end of a luxurious bar.

But as he shifted to break the kiss, she reached up, threaded her fingers through his hair and held him in place. Her mouth opened to him, inviting a deeper kiss, even as her fingers pulled hard enough at his hair to pull out several strands.

He jerked back, laughed shortly and said, "Ow."

She blushed, bit down on her bottom lip and let her hand slide from the back of his head. "Sorry," she said, her voice a whisper of sound that tugged at his insides. "Guess you bring out the wild in me."

She was doing the same damn thing to him. Forget dinner. Forget getting to know each other. All he wanted at the moment was her under him. Over him. He'd never desired any woman so desperately as he did this one. And Jackson wasn't a man to deny himself.

"I like wild," he said and laid one hand on her knee, his fingertips sliding discreetly beneath the hem of that spectacular dress to touch her bare skin. "How wild are we talking?"

She took a breath, grabbed her clutch purse off the bar and dipped her hand inside as if she were looking for something. Then she snapped the bag closed again, lifted her gaze to his and said, "Um, I think maybe this was a mistake."

"I think you're wrong," he said and smiled to himself as she jumped a little at the touch of his fingertips moving across her thigh. "I think you *are* feeling a little wild tonight. And I know I am."

"Jackson…"

"Kiss me again."

"There are people here," she reminded him.

"Didn't bother you a second ago."

"Does now," she said.

"Ignore them," he coaxed. Not usually a man who liked an audience, he couldn't care less about the sprinkling of people in the bar. He didn't want to chance her cooling off, coming to her senses. He needed to kiss her again. To remind her what was sizzling between them. Besides, the lighting was so dim, and he and Casey were so far from anyone else, they might as well have been alone anyway. And right now, that was good enough.

Her gaze lifted to his and when he looked into her eyes, he saw her wavering. Good enough. Leaning in close to her again, he kept one hand on her leg, letting his fingers slide higher onto her thigh even as his mouth took hers again.

She inhaled sharply, deeply at the touch of his lips and an instant later, her inhibitions went out the window, just as he'd hoped they would. Her tongue tangled with his and when he leaned in closer, sliding his hand higher, she sighed into his mouth and shivered beneath his touch.

"Let's get out of here," he whispered, when he'd managed to take his mouth from hers.

"I can't."

"Yes we can," he said, fingers moving higher, higher up her thigh. She shifted instinctively, and he knew she was feeling the same burn he was. "I have a room upstairs."

"Oh…" She took a breath, blew it out and shook her head. "That's probably not a good idea."

"Trust me, it's the best idea I've had all day." Abruptly, Jackson reached for his wallet, threw a hundred-dollar bill onto the bar, then tucked the wallet away again and took one of her hands in his. "Come with me."

She looked up at him and even in the dim light, Jackson saw the sheen of something hot and needy in her eyes. She wasn't going to refuse him. A moment later, she proved him right.

Standing up, she grabbed her clutch bag off the bar, and let him lead her from the room. He walked quickly, wanting to reach the elevator before she changed her mind. She kept up with him, the sound of her heels tapping out a quick rhythm on the floor that sounded like a frantic heartbeat.

Jackson wasted no time. The elevator doors dinged and swished open and he pulled his mystery woman inside. Before the doors were shut again, he turned her back to the wall and kissed her. His tongue swept inside, tangled with hers and he felt her surrender even as she lifted both arms to hook them around his neck. She held him close and arched her body into his as he pressed tighter and tighter to her.

Again and again, he ravaged her mouth and as he did,

he shifted one hand, sliding up from her waist to cover one of her breasts. Even through the silky slide of the sapphire-blue fabric, he felt her erect nipple. Flicking its tender surface with his thumb, he listened to her moan and let that soft sound feed his own passions.

The doors opened again on the top floor and Jackson stepped back from her reluctantly. Her hair was a wild tumble, her eyes were glassy and her delicious mouth was puffy and swollen from his kisses. He wanted her desperately.

Heading down the hall, he opened the door to the suite that he kept, pulled her inside then slammed and locked the door again. In an instant, she was back in his arms.

No hesitation, no awkwardness, they came together as if they'd been touching each other for eternity. There were no games, only need. No shyness, only desire. No second thoughts, only a wild, frenzied passion blistering the air.

Jackson yanked the zipper of her dress and slid the shoulders and sleeves down her arms. He thanked whatever gods were listening that she wasn't wearing a bra. Her breasts were beautiful, just the right size and looked so tempting, he didn't wait another moment.

Covering them with his hands, he pulled and tweaked with her hardened nipples and listened to Casey's soft moans and whispers as if they were the sweetest music ever composed. He bent his head to taste first one erect bud and then the other and knew he had to have more of her.

Her hands at his shoulders tightened, holding him to her, even as she swayed from the impact of his actions.

"More," he murmured, his tongue circling her nipple. "All."

And he pushed her dress the rest of the way to the floor. It fell in a sapphire puddle at her feet and he helped her step out of it. Her fingers were at his suit coat now, shoving it off, then loosening his tie and tearing at the buttons of his shirt. His hands roamed over her amazing body, sliding over cool, lavender-scented skin again and again, as if he were trying to memorize every line, every curve.

Then her palms were on his naked chest and he felt the zing of heat slice into him. Quickly, he tore off the rest of his clothes, picked Casey up in his arms and carried her to the nearest flat surface. He wasn't going to wait another moment. He had to have her. Be in her. Had to know what it was like to be surrounded by her heat.

"Now," she whispered as he laid her down on the extra wide couch in the living room of the suite. She opened her legs for him, reached up her arms and in the pale wash of golden lamplight, her eyes burned an arctic blue. "Now, Jackson. I need…"

"Me too," he admitted, willing to let her know just how affected he was by her. No games. No secrets. For this woman, this moment, he wanted her to know that from the first moment she'd smiled at him from across the room, he'd been aching for this.

Then the talking was over and all that was left to be said was said by their bodies. He entered her with one hard thrust and she gasped, arching into him, silently demanding he go deeper, harder, faster.

He did.

Every move she made only fed his need. Every response quickened the fires inside. Every touch, every slide of skin to skin, every gasp and moan and sigh worked together to push him higher than he'd ever been before. And Jackson wanted more.

He looked into her eyes when he felt her climax nearing. He watched as pleasure flashed across her face. He heard her gasp, felt her body's tremors. Then she locked her legs around his hips to hold him tightly even as she rocked her hips and cried out his name.

Something inside Jackson burst wide open and seconds later, his body erupted, throwing him after her into the wild, surging storm.

Casey woke up in the middle of the night. Her body felt sore and stiff and, she silently admitted, fabulous. It had been a *long* time since she'd had sex. She'd almost forgotten how good it could make you feel.

Until the guilt started seeping in.

She wasn't the one-night-stand kind of girl. She'd never done anything like this in her life and she was still trying to come to grips with the fact that she'd done it *now*.

Moonlight spilled into the hotel bedroom through the glass French doors leading to what she assumed was a balcony. She hadn't really had a chance to explore the suite, after all. She'd gone from the couch to the bed and that was about the sum total of her "tour."

God, Casey, what did you do?

Turning her head on the pillow, she looked at the sleeping man lying next to her. He was on his stomach, the silk duvet pulled up just over his hips. He had one arm stretched out toward her and Casey had to curl her fingers into her palms to keep from reaching out and smoothing his dark hair back from his forehead. In sleep, Jackson looked less dangerous, but hardly vulnerable.

There was still a hardness, a strength about him that seemed to resonate around him, even when sleeping. The man was a force of nature. She was lying there, naked and well used in his bed as a testament to that fact.

She hadn't planned to have sex with him.

Although, what they'd shared couldn't be called simply *sex*. Sex was just a biological function. At least, it always had been before that night. But what she'd shared with Jackson had gone way beyond anything she'd ever experienced before. Even now, hours after his last touch, her body was still humming. And that wasn't a good thing.

Because she wasn't looking for a relationship. Heck, she'd gotten what she'd come there for while they were still in the bar. How she'd allowed herself to end up in his bed was something she still wasn't sure about.

The only thing she was certain of, was that it was beyond time for her to leave. Best she do that before he woke up and tried to stop her. Quietly, stealthily, she slipped from the massive bed and the air in the room felt cool against her bare skin.

Moonlight lay across the silk duvet-covered mattress, spotlighting Jackson's broad, tanned, naked back in a silvery glow. He shifted in his sleep, and the duvet slid down his skin, revealing a paler swatch of flesh just below his waist. Casey took a breath and forced herself to look away. She didn't need to be tempted to stay. This was not part of her plan. She'd already gone too far. Allowed her hormones and her need to sweep away rational thought.

Tiptoeing across the moonlit bedroom like a naked burglar, she hurried into the living room of the luxurious suite and in the dim light, wasted several minutes trying to spot her clothes. But she didn't dare turn on a light. She didn't want to chance waking him up. Didn't want to risk him tempting her back into his arms. Into his bed.

"You are *such* an idiot," she whispered, hardly able to believe she'd let herself get into such a situation. She was usually so much more careful. Restrained, even.

When she spotted her discarded dress, Casey grabbed it up, hitched herself into it and clumsily worked the back zipper. Shouldn't these things be on the side? Finally, she was at least dressed—minus the panties that seemed to have disappeared. She picked up her heels and searched for her clutch bag. Finding it on the floor, half under the couch where she and Jackson had first come together. Swallowing hard, she avoided looking at the couch, snatched her purse and then headed for the front door.

She turned the knob carefully, opened the door and let the hallway light fall into the room in a narrow, golden slice. Before she stepped through the doorway though, Casey turned for one last look. She'd never been in a hotel room this elegant. She'd never been with a man like Jackson. In fact, this room, this man, were so far removed from her real life, that she felt like Cinderella at the end of the ball. The magic was over. The spell was ended.

She stepped into the hall, closed the door behind her and nearly ran to the elevator.

Time to get back to the real world.

Two

"Her name is Casey. She's about five foot five, has blond hair and blue eyes."

"Well," his assistant Anna Coric mused, "at least that narrows it down. Blue eyes, you say?"

"Funny." But Jackson wasn't laughing. He'd awakened to find himself alone and if the scent of lavender hadn't still been clinging to his skin, if he hadn't found a pair of white lace panties on the living room floor, he might have convinced himself that the hours with his mystery woman had never happened.

Why the hell would she leave without a word?

Anna, a middle-aged mother of four, worked for Jackson at the King family airfield. She kept ahead of the paperwork and made sure Jackson and the pilots who worked for him were always on top of their schedules. If the military had any sense at all, Jackson had often thought, they'd have hired mothers to be generals. Anna kept his work life running like a fine-tuned engine.

Too bad she couldn't do the same for his personal life.

He thought of something, snapped his fingers and said, "Wait. She said her full name was Cassiopeia. That should help you find her."

Anna glanced at him from the cabinet where she was deftly filing last month's flight plans, gas usage records and pilot hours. She paused in her work, turned amused brown eyes on him and said, "As much as it pleases me to know you think I'm a miracle worker, I'll need more than her first name and the color of her eyes to find her."

"Right."

"Besides," she said thoughtfully, "don't you have enough women in your life already?"

He chose to misunderstand her meaning and flashed her a smile. "You're right, Anna my love. You're more than enough woman for me."

She laughed, as he'd known she would. "Oh, you're smooth, Jackson. I give you that."

Smooth enough to have managed to change the subject before Anna could start reminding him of things he'd rather not think about at the moment.

Jackson left Anna to her work and walked into his private office. Here on the airstrip, there was a tower, of course, and a main building with a room for their wealthy passengers to wait for their planes in comfort. The boarding room was lavishly appointed with overstuffed sofas and chairs, reading material, plasma TV, plus a fully staffed bar and snack area. Above that main room, were the offices. One for Jackson, one for Anna and one room that was mainly storage.

Jackson's office, like Anna's, overlooked the airfield. The walls were a tinted glass that let in light but kept the glare down to a minimum. Also, Jackson had never liked being cooped up, and having walls of glass made him feel less like he was spending time in a box when he absolutely *had* to be in the office.

Normally, he preferred spending his time on the luxury jet fleet he owned and operated. Sure, he had a staff of pilots working for him, but he enjoyed the footloose lifestyle that running his own business provided. And the chance to fly superseded everything else in his mind. Practically took an act of Congress to get him to do paperwork, but he could fly rings around most other pilots and was happiest in the air.

Today though, he walked to his desk, sat down and deliberately ignored the view. "Casey. Casey *what?* And why the hell didn't you get her last name?"

Disgusted, he sat back in his leather desk chair and stared at the phone. This shouldn't be bothering him. Not like he wasn't used to one-night stands. But damn it, in the usual scheme of things *he* was the one who did the slipping away. He wasn't used to having a woman slink off in the middle of the night. He wasn't used to being the one left wondering what the hell had happened.

He had to say, he didn't care for it.

When the phone rang, he grabbed it, more to silence the damn noise than because he was in the mood for talking. "What is it?"

"You're damn cheerful this morning."

Jackson frowned at his brother's voice. "Travis. What's going on?"

"Just checking to make sure we're still on for dinner this weekend. Julie's got her mom lined up as a babysitter."

Despite his foul mood, Jackson smiled. In the last couple of years, he'd become an uncle. Twice over. First his oldest brother Adam and his wife Gina had become the parents of Emma, now a nearly unstoppable force of nature at a year and a half old. Then it was Travis and his wife Julie's turn. Their daughter Katie was just a few months old and already had taken over their household.

And though Jackson loved his nieces, after a visit with either of his brothers, he walked into his own quiet, peaceful house with a renewed sense of gratitude. Nothing like being around proud parents and babies to make a man appreciate being single.

"Yeah," he said, sitting up to lean one arm on his desktop. What with his mystery woman, an upcoming flight to Maine and a plane in for a refit, Jackson had almost forgotten about his dinner date with the family. "We're still on. We've got reservations at Serenity. Eight o'clock. Figured we could meet in the bar for drinks around seven. That work for you?"

"It's fine. Will Marian be joining us?"

Jackson frowned. "Don't see why she should. She's not part of the family."

"She will be."

"I haven't proposed to her yet, Travis."

"But you're still going to."

"Yeah." He'd made the decision more than a month ago. Marian Cornice, only daughter of Victor Cornice, a man who owned many of the country's largest private airfields.

Joining their families was a business decision, pure and simple. Once he was married to Marian, King Jets would grow even larger. With unlimited access to so many new airports, he'd be able to expand faster than his original business plan had allowed. The Cornice family was wealthy, but compared to the King family fortune, they were upstarts. In the marriage, Marian got the King name and fortune, plus she pleased her father, who admittedly was the spearhead of this match, and Jackson got the airfields. A win-win situation for everyone. Besides, both of his brothers had entered into marriages of convenience and they'd made them work. Why should he be any different?

If an image of his mystery woman floated into his mind, Jackson told himself it was fine because he wasn't officially engaged yet. Wasn't as if he were cheating on Marian.

"If you're seriously going to do this, marry her I mean, it would be a chance for Marian to get used to the family," Travis pointed out. "But if you'd rather not, fine. I'll tell Adam about dinner. I'm driving Julie to the ranch so she and Gina and the kids can spend the day together."

"Man." Jackson shook his head and laughed a little. "Did you ever picture yourself a father, Travis? Because I've got to say, it's weird for me to think of you and Adam as being *dads.*"

"It's weird to be one too," Travis admitted, but Jackson

could hear the smile in his voice, even over the phone. "A good kind of weird, though. You should try it."

He snorted. "Never gonna happen, big brother."

"Marian might change your mind."

"Not likely." Jackson leaned back into his chair again. "She's not exactly the maternal type. Fine by me anyway. I can be the world's greatest uncle, spoil your kids rotten, then send them home."

"Mistakes happen," Travis said. "Everybody gets surprised once in awhile."

Okay, Travis and Julie hadn't been trying to have a baby, but Jackson wouldn't make the same mistakes. "When it comes to that sort of thing, I'm Mister Careful. I'm so careful I'm practically covered head to toe in plastic wrap. I'm—" A hideous thought flashed through his mind, jolting him from his chair to his feet.

"You're mistake-proof, I get it...." Travis prodded, waited for a response and when he didn't get one said, "Jackson? You okay?"

"Fine," he muttered, already hanging up when he added, "Gotta go. Bye."

Careful?

He hadn't been careful the night before. Hell, he hadn't even thought of careful until just this minute. Last night, he'd been too caught up in the woman with blue eyes and a luscious mouth. Last night, he'd let himself get lost in the urgency of the moment.

For the first time in years, he hadn't used a condom.

Jackson muttered a curse, kicked the bottom drawer of his desk and ignored the slam of pain that rocketed from his foot up his leg. Served him right if he'd broken something. How could he have been so stupid? Not only hadn't he been careful, but he'd been with a stranger. A woman he knew nothing about. A woman who, for all he knew, had deliberately set up the situation to try to get pregnant by one of the wealthy King family.

He shoved one hand through his dark brown hair, then stuffed that hand into the pocket of his black jeans. Every muscle was tensed. His back teeth ground together and he told himself that no matter how difficult this turned out to be, he had to find that woman.

Casey.

Had to find her, discover who the hell she was and what she'd been up to the night before.

Still furious with himself, he stared out the window at the view stretching in front of him. A few of the King Jets were lined up on the tarmac, their deep blue paint shining, their tail fins proudly displaying the stylized gold crown that was the King family logo. Usually, his sense of pride swelled when he looked down on those jets. On the empire he'd taken over at twenty-five and built into one of the most enviable in the world.

Now, as he stared, unseeing, one of those jets roared down the runway, tore into the sky and lifted off to sail into the clouds.

While Jackson stood, earthbound, feeling like he was sinking deeper and deeper into a mire.

He had to find her. Especially now. He couldn't risk losing this merger with the Cornice family.

And he sure as hell wasn't ready to become a father.

* * *

A week later, Casey held the phone in a grip so tight her knuckles were white. "You're sure? There's no mistake?"

"Honey, I checked and rechecked." Casey's best friend Dani Sullivan's voice came through loud and clear with just a touch of sympathy. "There's no mistake."

"I knew it." Casey sighed, leaned back against the kitchen wall and stared up at the rooster clock hanging on the wall opposite her. The hands went to five o'clock and the rooster crowed. Why had she ever bought such a ridiculous clock? Who needed a rooster crowing every hour on the hour?

And who cared about the stupid rooster?

"Thanks for putting a rush on this, Dani." Dani worked full-time at a private lab and she'd done the testing herself, just so Casey could not only get the results faster, but be absolutely sure about those results. "I appreciate it."

"No problem sweetie," she said. "But what are you going to do now?"

"Only one thing I can do," Casey said, straightening up and walking across the room to grab her iced tea off the kitchen counter. The old fashioned wall phone's cord was stretched to its limits and slowly reeled Casey back in. "I've got to go see him."

"Hmm," Dani said thoughtfully, "considering what happened the last time you went to see him face-to-face, maybe you should consider a phone call instead."

"You're never going to let me forget that, are you?" The whole point of a best friend was having someone you could tell your deepest, darkest secrets to. So naturally, she'd spilled her guts to Dani. The downside was, Dani wasn't shy about offering her opinion.

"The point is, you haven't forgotten it, have you?"

"No," Casey said. She hadn't forgotten. Worse, she'd dreamed of Jackson almost every night. She kept waking up hot and flushed, with the memory of his hands on her skin. And that memory, rather than fading, was only getting stronger. With only a small effort, she could almost taste his kiss again.

And she didn't want to admit just how often she expended that effort.

"But," she said, lifting her chin before taking a sip of her tea, hoping the icy drink would cool her off a little, "that doesn't mean I'd make the same mistake again. Once bitten and all that."

"Uh-huh."

"You know, a little support wouldn't be out of line," Casey said, frowning.

"Oh, I'm supportive," Dani argued, her voice low enough that no one else who worked with her could overhear, "but I still don't think it's a good idea for you to meet him face-to-face, so to speak, again. With the kind of news you're going to deliver, I really think you'd be better off making a phone call from a safe distance."

Probably. But she couldn't do that. She really resented being put in this position, but there was nothing she could do about it now. By all rights, Casey never should have had to make this decision. Things had changed though and she'd been backed into a corner. So there was really only one thing to do. The right thing.

"Nope," she said. "I have to tell him. And I have to do it while I'm looking at him."

"Never could change your mind once it was made up," Dani muttered.

"True."

"Just be careful, okay?" her friend said. "He's one of the Kings, you know. They practically own half of California. If he decides to, he could make your life really difficult."

Fear curled in the pit of Casey's stomach. She'd considered that already. But she'd done her homework. She'd done research on Jackson. She knew he was the playboy type. The footloose and fancy-free kind of man. The kind who didn't want entanglements.

So she was pretty sure that despite the news she had to deliver, he wasn't going to make trouble for her. He'd probably thank her for the information, offer to write her a check—as if she'd take money for this—and then quietly go back to his lifestyle of easy women and mega money.

"He won't," Casey said firmly, wondering if she were trying to convince herself or Dani.

"I hope you're right," her friend said. "Because you're certainly betting a lot on the outcome of this."

Oh, Casey was well aware of that.

Three

Jackson looked across the table at the woman he was planning to marry and felt the slightest buzz of interest for her. But compared to what he had felt for his mystery woman, it was the voltage of a double A battery alongside the frenzied energy of a nuclear power plant.

He'd assumed that whatever attraction there was between them would grow with time. Hadn't happened yet though and he was forced again to remember the instant chemical reaction between he and Casey Whoever during their one night together. And what kind of statement was it that he'd had a better time with a perfect stranger than he was having with the woman he was expected to propose to? Images of Casey smiling, Casey naked, reaching for him, filled his mind and despite everything, Jackson felt his body burn and his chest tighten.

His mystery woman.

What had she been after?

She'd deliberately seduced him. Gone out of her way to entice him, then disappeared without a backward look. Who did that? And why?

If he didn't get answers soon, he was going to go nuts.

"My father says you're interested in the airstrip in upstate New York," Marian said, snapping Jackson's focus back to her.

As it should be. Didn't he have the damned engagement ring in his pocket? Wasn't he planning on proposing tonight? He had plans for his life and they didn't include mystery women, so best for him to get on with this.

"Yes, it's big enough for several flights a day and I've already worked out a new schedule with my pilots," he said, lifting his coffee cup for a sip. Dinner was over and there was only dessert left on the table. Naturally, Marian would no more eat the chocolate mousse she'd ordered than she would dance naked on the tabletop.

If there was one thing Jackson had learned about the woman over the last couple of months, it was that she was far more interested in how things looked than how things really were. She was painfully thin and ate almost nothing whenever they went out. And yet, she always ordered heartily, then spent her time pushing the food around on her plate with her fork.

His mystery woman, he recalled, had had curves. A body designed to allow a man to sink into her softness, cradle himself in her warmth.

Damn it.

Marian was watching him through calm brown eyes. Her dark brown hair was tucked into a knot on the back of her neck and her long-sleeved, high-necked black dress made her look even thinner and less approachable than usual. Why was he suddenly looking at Marian with different eyes?

And why couldn't he stop?

The small velvet box in the pocket of his suit coat felt as if it were on fire. Its presence was a constant reminder of what he was there to do and yet, he hadn't quite been able to bring himself to ask the question Marian was no doubt waiting to hear.

When he felt the vibration of his cell phone, Jackson reached for it gratefully. "Sorry," he said. "Business."

She nodded and Jackson glanced at the screen. He didn't recognize the number, but flipped the phone open anyway and said, "Jackson King."

"This is Casey."

His heart jumped in his chest. Even if she hadn't identified herself, he would have recognized that voice. He'd been hearing it in his sleep for days. But how the hell had she gotten this number? A question for another time. He shot a quick look at Marian, watching him, then keeping his own voice low and level, he said, "I've been wanting to talk to you."

"Now's your chance," she said and he heard the hesitation in her tone. "I'm at Drake's coffee shop on Pacific Coast Highway."

"I know the place."

"We need to talk. How soon can you get here?"

Jackson looked at Marian again and felt a small stab of relief at being able to escape this dinner and avoid asking the question he'd come there to ask. "Give me a half hour."

"Fine." She hung up instantly.

Jackson closed his phone, tucked it into his pocket and looked at the woman opposite him.

"Trouble?" she asked.

"A bit," he said, grateful she wasn't going to demand explanations. No doubt she was used to her father bolting out of dinners to take care of business. Reaching into his wallet, he pulled out the money required for the bill and a hefty tip. Then he stood up and asked, "I'll take you home first."

"Not necessary," she said, lifting her coffee cup for a sip. "I'll finish my coffee and get myself home."

That didn't set well. Bad enough he was leaving her to go meet another woman. The least he could do was see her home. But Marian had a mind of her own.

"Don't be foolish, Jackson. I'm perfectly capable of calling a cab. Go. Take care of business."

He shouldn't have felt relief, but he did. Another small tidal wave of it splashing through him. "All right then. I'll call you tomorrow."

She nodded, but he'd already turned to weave his way through the diners seated at linen-draped tables. He hardly noticed his surroundings. His mind was already fixed on the coming meeting. He would finally see his mystery woman again. Finally discover just what she'd been up to when she'd come onto him. He'd find out if she'd been protected during their night together.

And if she played her cards right, maybe the two of them could share another night of amazing sex.

Forty-five minutes later, he was parked outside Drake's. The place was practically an institution in this part of California. Around for more than fifty years, Drake's was cheap, the food was good and they never closed.

A far cry from the quiet dignity of the restaurant he'd just left, when Jackson pulled the door to Drake's open, he was met by a cacophony of sound. Conversations, laughter, a baby's cry. Silverware being jangled into trays and the crash of dirty plates swept into buckets by harried busboys. The overhead lighting was bright to the point of glaring and the hostess, inspecting her nail polish, looked just as bright when she spotted Jackson.

He hardly noticed though. Instead, his gaze swept over the booths and tables until he found the person he was looking for. Blond hair, pale cheeks, and blue eyes focused on him.

"Thanks," he said, walking past the hostess, "I found my table."

Walking down the crowded, narrow aisle between booths, he kept his gaze locked with Casey's and tried to read the emotions flashing one after the other across her features. But there were too many and they changed too quickly.

His gut fisted. Something was definitely up.

Tonight, she wasn't dressed to seduce. Tonight, she wore a pale green, long-sleeved T-shirt and her short hair was mussed, as if she'd been running her fingers through it. She wore small silver stars in her ears and was chewing at her bottom lip.

Nerves?

She should be nervous, he told himself. He had a few things to say to her and he doubted she was going to like many of them. But damn, just looking at her made him hot and hard again. She had a way of getting to him like no other woman ever had. Not something he wanted to admit even to himself, let alone her. But it was there. A niggling tug of desire that was damned hard to ignore. He stopped alongside her table, opened his mouth to speak and then slammed it shut again.

Beside her in the red vinyl booth, was a child's booster seat. And in that seat was a baby girl. Jackson scowled as the infant—surely not even a year old yet—turned her face up to his and grinned, displaying two tiny white teeth.

And *his* eyes.

Tearing his gaze from the child, Jackson glared at Casey and ground out, "Just what the *hell* is going on?"

For just a moment, Casey wondered if Dani hadn't been right. Maybe she should have just told him her news over the phone. At least then, she wouldn't be faced with a tall, gorgeous furious male looking at her as if she'd dropped down from the moon.

Casey had watched him arrive. Watched him approach, in his thousand-dollar suit, looking as out of place at Drake's as a picnic basket at a five-star restaurant. He'd obviously been out when she called. And she couldn't help wondering who he'd been with.

Now, she stared up into his eyes—the same eyes she saw every morning when her daughter woke up to smile at her—and fought down the nerve-induced churning in the pit of her stomach. She'd known he'd be angry and she was prepared for that. Didn't mean she had to like it.

Yes, she was doing the right thing. The only thing she could do, being the kind of person she was. But that didn't mean she wanted to. Or that she was feeling at all easy about this confrontation.

She watched as he shifted his gaze from her to the baby and back again and felt his tension mount. She didn't need to see it in the hard set of his broad shoulders or the tight clenching of his jaw. She could *feel* it, radiating out around him, like flames looking for fresh tinder.

And things were only going to get worse in the next few minutes.

"Why don't you sit down, Jackson?" she finally said, waving one hand at the bench seat opposite her. *Keep calm,* she told herself. *You're two mature adults. This can be settled quickly and calmly.*

As if he'd just remembered that they were in public, he grudgingly slid into the booth, braced his forearms on the table and glared at her.

Maybe not calmly. But at least he wasn't willing to shout and argue in public. Precisely why she'd chosen Drake's to let him in on her little secret. "Thanks for coming."

"Oh, are we being polite now?" He shook his head and let his gaze slide to the baby, now happily gumming the corner of a teething biscuit.

Casey knew what he was seeing. A beautiful little girl with a thatch of dark brown curls and big brown eyes. Her cheeks were rosy from the nap she'd taken on the drive to the diner and her smile was wide and delighted with the world.

But Jackson didn't look so delighted. He looked more like he'd been hit over the head with a two-by-four. Casey could hardly blame him for being shocked. Her daughter was the best thing that had ever happened to Casey. But Jackson was being slapped with a reality that she had been living with for nearly two years.

It was a lot to take in.

Especially for someone like him.

According to her very detailed research into his background, he was a womanizer. Hence her seduction routine at the bar a week ago. She'd known that he'd respond to her if she showed the slightest interest. It was what he did. He was a man who couldn't make a commitment that lasted more than a few weeks. He was dedicated to his own pleasure and living his life unencumbered.

Not exactly prime father material.

When his gaze shifted back to hers, Casey stiffened. Accusation and reproach shone in his eyes and were very hard to miss.

"Since we're being so very civil, you want to explain to me just what exactly is going on here?"

"That's why I called you. To explain."

"Start with how you got my cell number," he said and nodded when a waitress approached with a pot of coffee. She deftly turned the cup over on its saucer, poured the coffee, then drifted away again at his dismissive glance.

"I called your office at the King airfield," she said once they were alone again. "The recording on the answering machine listed your cell number for emergencies. I thought this qualified."

He blew out a breath, took a sip of his coffee, then set the cup down gingerly, as if he didn't trust himself not to throw it against a wall. "All right. Now, how about you explain the rest. Starting with your full name."

"Casey Davis."

"Where you from?"

"I live just outside Sacramento. A little town called Darby."

He nodded. "Okay. Now, about…" He glanced at the baby again.

Casey inhaled deeply, hoping to settle the jangle of nerves rattling around inside her. She'd known this was going to be hard. She just hadn't expected to feel almost mute when the time came for her to speak.

Clearing her throat, she told herself to just say it. So she reached over and smoothed her palm over the back of her daughter's head. "This is Mia. She's almost nine months old—" she paused to look deeply into his eyes "—and she's your daughter."

"I don't have children." His eyes narrowed until they were nothing more than slits with dark brown daggers shining through. After several long seconds ticked past, he finally said, "I don't know what you're trying to pull here, but it won't work. I've never seen you before a week ago."

"I know—"

He laughed shortly but there was no humor in the sound. The harsh overhead lights spilled down over him and weirdly cast his features more into shadow than illuminating them. "I came here wanting to find out who you were, why you slipped out on me and to find out if you were trying to set me up by getting pregnant deliberately…turns out you were way ahead of me."

Casey straightened up, insulted to the bone. She was trying to do the right thing and he thought she'd— "I was doing no such thing."

"You purposely set out to seduce me that night."

"It wasn't difficult," she said reminding him easily that she hadn't exactly kidnapped him, tied him to the bed and had her wicked way with him. But at the first memory of that night, her body stirred despite her best efforts.

"Not the point." He waved one hand as if dismissing that argument. "You had an agenda and saw it through. What I want to know, is *why?*"

Picking up a napkin, she leaned over, wiped Mia's mouth despite her daughter's efforts to pull free. Then Casey looked at Jackson again. "I went there to get a sample of your DNA."

He laughed again. Louder. Harsher. "You went a hell of a long way to collect it!"

She flushed and she knew it. She could feel heat staining her cheeks and hated the fact that she'd never been able to keep from doing that when she was embarrassed. Glancing around the diner, she made sure the other customers weren't paying them the slightest bit of attention before she said in a vicious whisper, "I took strands of your *hair.* Remember when you kissed me—"

"You kissed *me* as I remember it," he interrupted.

That's right. She had. All part of the plan that had taken a seriously wrong turn almost instantly after her mouth had touched his. And there was the uncomfortable twist and burn inside her. "Fine. I kissed you. Remember I pulled on your hair?"

"Ah yes," he said, leaning back into the seat and folding his arms over his chest. "You were feeling *wild,* you said."

"Yes, well." She shifted in her seat and wished she could get up and move around. She'd always thought better when she was walking. But she couldn't very well spring out of the booth while Mia was there, strapped into a booster seat. "I needed a follicle of your hair so I could have it tested."

"Why not simply ask?"

Now she laughed. "Sure. I'm going to go up to a strange man and ask for a sample of his DNA."

"Instead, you went up to a strange man and kissed him?"

Frowning, she admitted, "It seemed like a good idea at the time."

"And what about the rest of it?" he asked. "Was that part of your plan, too? Spend the night with me to what? Trap me into something somehow? Get me so wound up that neither one of us was considering any kind of protection?"

She cringed a little. She hadn't even thought of protection that night. The way she remembered it, she'd been so hot, so needy, so completely over the edge with a kind of desire she'd never known before, the thought of condoms hadn't even entered her head. And just how stupid was *that?*

"I didn't plan any of that," she said firmly. "The rest of that night just…happened." Her gaze snapped to his. "And while we're on the subject, I'd like to assure you that I'm perfectly healthy. I hope *you* can say the same."

"Yes. I am."

One worry taken care of, she told herself.

"That's good."

"And what about the other concern?" He asked the question slowly, as if judging her reaction.

"You mean pregnancy?"

He tipped his head toward Mia. "You seem to be fertile enough, it's a reasonable question."

"You don't have to worry," she told him. "The doctors say I would have a difficult time conceiving in the usual way."

One dark eyebrow lifted and she squirmed a little. Her personal history was just that. Personal. It wasn't something she discussed with just anyone.

"And yet…"

Again, he nodded toward Mia, gurgling and now slapping that teething biscuit against the tabletop.

"Look," he said, capturing her attention again, "let's leave everything else for the moment and go back to the real matter at hand." He glanced at Mia and Casey wanted to hide her daughter from his appraising gaze. "You needed my DNA. Why? We'd never met. How could you think I'm the father of your child?"

More personal history that she would prefer not to discuss. Yet, she'd come here tonight because she'd felt she didn't have a choice.

"Nearly two years ago," she said, her voice low enough that no one could possibly overhear her, "I went to the Mandeville clinic…"

She saw understanding dawn on his features. His eyes opened, his firm mouth relaxed a little and his gaze, when it shifted to Mia, was this time, more stunned than angry or suspicious.

"The sperm bank," he muttered.

"Yes." Casey shifted in her seat a little, uncomfortable discussing this with anyone, let alone the "donor" who'd made her daughter's birth possible.

He shook his head, scrubbed one hand across his face and said, "That's just not possible."

"Clearly," she said, "it is."

"No, you don't understand." His gaze locked on hers again, silently demanding an explanation for how this could have happened. "Yes, in college, I admit, I went to the clinic with a friend of mine. We'd lost a bet and—"

"A bet?"

He frowned at her. "Anyway, I went, made the donation and didn't think about it again until about five years ago. I realized that I didn't want a child of mine, unknown to me, growing up out there somewhere. I told them I wanted that sample destroyed."

A chill swept through her at those words. She glanced at her daughter and as a wave of love rushed through her, she tried to imagine a life without Mia in it. And couldn't. Somehow, through some bureaucratic mishap, Jackson's order had gotten lost in the shuffle, overlooked and ignored. She could only be grateful. Knowing how close she'd come to never having Mia only made her treasure her daughter even more.

She smiled. "Well, I'm glad to say they didn't do as you requested."

"Obviously."

It wasn't hard to judge his current feelings. He was now avoiding looking at Mia at all. And that was fine with Casey. She didn't want him interested in her daughter. Mia was *hers*. Her family. Casey was only here because she'd felt that Jackson had a right to know he had a child.

"I thought sperm banks were anonymous," he said a moment later.

"They're supposed to be." When she'd gone to the Mandeville clinic, she'd specifically made sure that she would never know the identity of her child's father. She wasn't looking for a relationship, after all. She didn't need a partner to help her raise a child. All she'd wanted was a baby to love. A family of her own.

When she was assured that their donors' identities were very strictly protected, Casey'd been relieved. And that relief had stayed with her until about a month ago.

"I got an e-mail almost four weeks ago," she said softly. "From the Mandeville clinic. It listed my name, the donor number I'd selected and identified you as the man who'd made the original deposit."

He winced a little at that.

"Naturally, I was furious. This whole thing was supposed to be anonymous, remember. I called the clinic to complain," she told him and with the memories flooding her mind, she felt again that helpless sense of betrayal she'd experienced when she first read that e-mail. "They were in a panic. It seems someone hacked into their computers and sent out dozens of e-mails to women identifying the fathers of their children. It wasn't supposed to happen, of course, but it was too late to change anything."

"I see."

Two words, said so tightly it was a wonder he'd been able to squeeze them out of his throat. Well, fine. Casey understood that this was a surprise. But he had to understand that she wasn't happy about this, either.

"I didn't want to know the name of my daughter's father," she said firmly. "I wasn't interested in the man then and I'm not interested now. I didn't go to a sperm bank looking for a lasting connection, after all. All I wanted was a baby."

A muscle in his jaw twitched and an emotional shutter was down over his eyes, preventing her from getting the slightest impression of what he was thinking. "And you found this out a month ago."

"Yes."

He tapped his fingertips against the table. "Why'd you wait so long to tell me?"

Though his tone was even, his voice quiet, Casey had no problem identifying the anger behind that statement.

She took a gulp of her now cold coffee and grimaced as it slid down her throat. "Frankly, I'd considered not telling you at all at first."

His eyebrows arched.

"But soon enough, I realized you had the right to know if you actually *were* Mia's father."

"You doubted it?"

"Why wouldn't I?" she countered. "Just because some hacker got into the clinic's computer system doesn't mean he did a good job of it." Then she looked him straight in the eye. "Besides, you are definitely not the kind of father

I wanted for my baby. When I went to Mandeville, I specifically requested the sperm of a *scientist*."

For a second, insult flashed across his face, then he snorted a laugh again and shook his head as if he couldn't believe they were even having this conversation. "A scientist?"

"I wanted my child to be smart."

He glared at her. "I graduated magna cum laude."

"With a degree in partying? Or women?"

"I happen to have an MBA, not that it's any of your business."

She had already known that, thanks to her research, but the point was, she knew very well what Jackson King considered most important in his life. And it wasn't intellectual pursuits.

"It doesn't really matter anymore," Casey said with a sigh. "I love my daughter and I don't care who her father is."

"Yet, as soon as you found out her father was Jackson King," he countered, "you came to me. So what's this little meeting really about?"

"I beg your pardon?" She sounded as stuffy as her late aunt Grace.

"You heard me, Casey Davis. You came here to present me with my daughter—"

"*My* daughter," she corrected, wondering why this conversation was suddenly feeling like more than a verbal battle.

"So it makes a man wonder, just what it is you really want from me? Money?" He reached into the breast pocket of his suit and pulled out a black leather wallet. "How much are you after? Looking for some child support? Is that what this is about?"

"That is just typical," she said, feeling a slow burn of anger start to build within. "Of course you think this is about money. That's how you see the world, isn't it? Well, I already told you, I don't want anything from you."

"I don't believe you."

She hissed in a breath and devoutly wished she'd never told him about Mia. "You can think whatever you like. I can't stop you. But I can leave. This little conversation is over."

Turning in her seat, she unstrapped her baby from the booster chair, lifted Mia into her arms and cuddled her close as she scooted out of the booth. Feeling Mia's warmth against her was a soothing balm to the anger churning inside her. It didn't matter what Jackson King thought or did. She'd done the right thing, now she could put him behind her. She could concentrate on her daughter.

When she was standing, her purse hanging from her shoulder to slap against her jean-clad thigh, Casey looked down at Jackson. And this time there was pity in her eyes. Because he couldn't grasp just how much he was missing, not knowing the child he'd helped create.

"I thought you had a right to know that you'd helped make this beautiful little girl possible, whether or not it was done willingly," she said, disgust pumping into her words. "But I can see now that was a mistake. Don't worry though, Jackson. Mia will never know that her father thought so little of her."

"Is that right?" He smiled up at her, clearly believing her outrage just another part of the act. "What will you tell her about me?"

"I'll tell her you're dead," Casey said quietly. "Because as far as I'm concerned, you are."

Four

She moved fast, he'd give her that.

But then, shock had slowed him down a little, too.

Jackson was only a step or two behind her, raw emotion pumping through his system. He couldn't even believe what was happening. At thirty-one years old, he was a father. To a little girl who'd been alive for nearly a year and he hadn't known it. What the hell was a man supposed to do with information like that?

His gaze fixed on Casey as she hurried across the parking lot and even as furious as he was, he couldn't stop himself from admiring the rear view of her. Her jeans clung to her behind and her legs like a second skin and instantly, lust roared up inside and kept time with the anger frothing in his gut.

Casey was already at her car, putting the baby into a car

seat when he caught up with her. A cold ocean wind slapped at him as he approached, almost as if someone, somewhere was trying to keep him at a distance.

Well the hell with that.

"You can't just drop this bomb on me, then walk away."

She flipped her head around, froze him with a hard look and muttered, "Watch me."

He glanced at the baby, who was watching them both through wide brown eyes. After being around his nieces for several months, Jackson recognized the expression on the baby's face. The tiny girl looked confused and on the verge of tears. Not what he wanted. So he lowered his voice, tried to force a smile into place and said, "Look, you surprised me. Sandbagged me. And I think you know it."

Casey paid no attention to him, instead, she struggled with the straps on the car seat. "This stupid thing always gives me fits."

He didn't want to talk about the car seat. Getting more impatient by the minute, he finally took hold of Casey's arm, ignored the instant sizzle that touching her caused, pulled her back and said "Let me do it."

She laughed. "How do *you* know anything about infant car seats?"

"I have two nieces," he muttered, not bothering to glance at her.

He'd had plenty of practice over the last year, dealing with all of the accoutrements that seemed to come along with a baby. Emma had more luggage than her parents and in a few short months, Katie's toys and necessities had completely taken over the vineyard.

In seconds, he had the buckles snapped securely. He looked at *his daughter* and tried to wrap his brain around that simple fact. Didn't work. Still, he traced one finger down the baby's cheek and got a giggle for his trouble. His heart ached with a completely unfamiliar feeling as he looked into eyes so like his own.

When he backed out of the car, he was still smiling until he caught the fiery look in Casey's eyes.

"Thanks," she said quickly, then pushed past him to close the car door and walk around to the driver's seat.

Jackson stayed right at her heels. Before she could open her car door and escape him, he grabbed hold of her arm again. "Just wait a damn minute, all right?"

She pulled free of his grasp and he let her go. Shoving one hand through his hair, he took a breath, glanced around at the full parking lot and then looked back at her. "I don't know what you want from me."

"Nothing," she said and now she sounded almost tired. "I've already said that. Now I have to go."

He slapped one hand against the car door and held it shut. Bending down, he looked directly into her blue eyes and said, "You've known about the baby—"

"Mia—"

"—Mia," he corrected, "for nearly two years. I've known for—" he checked his watch. "Ten minutes. Maybe you could cut me a break here, huh? It's not every day a man finds out he's a father while sitting in a twenty-four-hour diner that smells of corned beef hash."

An all-too-brief smile curved her mouth then disappeared again in a heartbeat.

Jackson's mind was racing. He'd just received the biggest news of his life. How the hell was he supposed to react?

"Fine," she said and he could see that the effort to be reasonable was costing her. "You need time. Take all the time you want. Take *eternity* if you need to." Her gaze bored into his. "While you get used to the idea, Mia and I will go back to our lives."

"Just like that?"

She jerked him a nod and the silver stars in her ears winked at him, reflecting off the parking lot lights. "Just like that. You needed to know, now you do. That's all."

He looked through the car windows at the back of the car seat. He couldn't see Mia's face, but he didn't have to. The image was burned into his memory. He doubted he would ever forget his first look at her.

Something momentous had just happened to him and damned if he could make sense of it standing in a crowded parking lot. So he'd let Casey go. Let her take his daughter away.

For now.

She'd find out soon enough that he wasn't a man to be dismissed whenever she felt it was time.

"All right. Take Mia home." Easing off the car, Jackson stepped aside and allowed her to open the door. He noticed the wary suspicion in her eyes, but didn't care to say anything that might ease it. Let her worry a bit. She'd put him through the wringer in a matter of a few minutes. Worrying about it now was the least she could do.

She tossed her purse onto the front passenger seat, curled her fingers over the top of the car door and looked at him. In the dim light, her deep blue eyes were shadowed. A trick of the night? Or something else?

"I guess this is goodbye," she said and mustered up a smile that only managed to tip one corner of her mouth. "I don't suppose we'll be seeing each other again, so have a nice life, Jackson."

He watched her leave, memorized her license plate number and was already making plans as he headed to his car.

"It went great," Casey lied as she moved around her kitchen, entangling herself in the phone cord as she went. She really had to get a cordless for this room. Opening the refrigerator door, she pulled out a bottle of chardonnay then went for a wineglass. "He saw Mia, we talked, then we came home and he went…wherever men like him go."

Mia was sound asleep in her room, the house was quiet and Casey was still a bundle of nerves. Seeing Jackson again had been way too hard. She hadn't expected the sexual tug to be as strong as before. And then, watching his face as he looked at Mia and realized the truth had really sucker punched her. He'd looked stunned, of course. But there was an undercurrent, too. A look of a man glimpsing something he'd never expected to find. Like he'd stumbled across a treasure—just before his eyes went cold and calculating again.

And that worried her a little.

After all, as Dani had pointed out, the King family was a powerful force in California. What if he decided to take Mia from Casey? Then what? No, she told herself instantly. He'd signed a form when he donated his sperm, giving up all rights to a baby. Though with his family's power, he could probably negate that form. He wasn't interested in having a child.

Instead, he'd actually thought Casey had come to him for money!

Was that really how he looked at the world around him? Everything solved by a checkbook or a thick wallet? Did he really believe that she would use her *daughter* to make money? What kind of horrible people did he know, anyway?

"Uh-huh," Dani said. "Your voice sounds filled with all kinds of good feelings and happy butterflies."

"Okay," she admitted, "no happy butterflies. Should have known I couldn't put one past you." Casey poured the sunlight-colored wine into a glass, recorked the bottle and only then noticed the label. *Kings Vineyard.* Perfect. Even when he wasn't here, she was reminded of Jackson. Not that she needed reminding.

She could almost feel him right now, as she stood, safe in her tiny kitchen. The man's inherent strength and *presence* was something that lingered. At least, it did in her case.

"It wasn't great and it wasn't easy. He was stunned and not in a happy way." Casey nodded firmly, forced herself to put a good spin on the night by adding, "But it ended well. I came home with Mia and Jackson went away."

"Permanently?" Dani asked.

"I hope so," Casey admitted. "He said he needed time to adjust. I told him we don't want anything from him, but I'm not sure he heard me. Either way though, the point is, mission accomplished. I told him, it's over now, and I can go back to my life. Put this all behind me."

"And you really think it's going to be that easy?" Dani paused, half covered the phone receiver and said, "Mikey, don't run the choo-choo train on your sister's head. That's a good boy."

Casey grinned. Trust Dani and her wild bunch to keep things in perspective. "Having trouble?"

"Nice subject change," Dani told her with a laugh. "And the answer is yes. I love my husband, don't get me wrong, but when Mike's in charge, the kids pretty much rule the house. When it's my turn, I spend most of my time in damage control."

Dani's husband Mike, a Darby police officer, worked nights and Dani worked days. That way, there was always a parent around for the kids. A tired parent, but at least the children were cared for by family. Of course, Dani insisted it had been so long since she'd had sex, she only had a vague recollection of it.

Casey's memories on the other hand, were clear and vivid. Which was just part of the problem.

"I don't know how you take care of Mia all alone," Dani said, switching the subject back to Casey. "I mean, Mike and I have separate shifts, but we always know there's somebody to back us up. To turn to. To *whine* to."

Casey smiled a little wistfully. She'd known going in, that she and her child would be alone. And that was okay with her most of the time. If she sometimes envied Dani's relationship with her husband, she figured that was only normal.

"I've never known it any other way," she admitted,

putting the wine bottle back in the fridge and picking up her glass for a sip. "When I decided to get pregnant, I knew I'd be doing it alone. Sure, there's nobody to help out, but I don't have to share her with anyone either."

"You don't just share the bad stuff, Casey," Dani said. "It's nice to have someone to turn to and say, 'Hey, did you just see that? Isn't our kid brilliant?'"

Casey lifted her chin. "I have you to call and brag to. Besides, Mia and I get along great."

"I love you and Mia like crazy, you know that. And nobody's saying you're not doing great on your own."

"But? I hear a but in there somewhere."

"Okay, *but*," Dani said. "I think you're being unrealistic to believe that Jackson King is going to disappear just because you want him to."

Casey's stomach did a quick flip and she took another sip of wine. She didn't want to believe her friend, but hadn't she been thinking the same thing earlier, while she'd bathed Mia and put her to bed?

Jackson came from a wealthy, powerful family. If he wanted to make trouble for her, he could. Right thing to do or not, she was beginning to wish she'd never contacted Jackson.

Casey dropped into one of the two wooden chairs pulled up to a tiny table in one corner of her kitchen. She stared out at the night beyond the windowpanes, where her postage-stamp-sized backyard lay and tried to keep panic at bay.

Shaking her head, she said, more to convince herself than Dani, "Why would he come back? He doesn't want a baby.

His whole lifestyle is built around hedonism. He does what he wants when he wants. He's got a home he rarely stays in, his business has him flying all over the world and he's not exactly a candidate for Mr. Commitment."

"That's the thing though, honey," Dani said softly. "He's never had a reason to commit to anything before, has he?"

"No. No, he hasn't." Casey set her wineglass down on the table and carefully unwrapped the curled phone cord from around her shoulders. "And by telling him the truth, I've just given him one, haven't I?"

The next morning, Jackson was at the King family ranch, having called an emergency family meeting. He faced both of his brothers and was grateful that neither one of them had brought their wives into this.

"Did you actually see the DNA report?" Adam asked.

Jackson stopped pacing the confines of the elegantly appointed room and shot his oldest brother a look. "No, I didn't."

"Well, why the hell not?" Travis demanded from his seat in a dark brown leather chair.

Shifting him a glare, Jackson snapped, "I was a little shocked, okay? Having a child you never knew existed thrown at you all of a sudden is more surprising than you might think. Besides, I don't need to see the report. You'll know what I mean when you see Mia. She looks just like Emma and Katie." He paused for effect, then added, "Prettier, of course, but then I'm the father."

Adam chuckled and shook his head. "You're sure taking this better than I thought you would."

"You should have seen me last night." Jackson had spent the entire night prowling through the home he rarely stayed in. The rooms were empty, the caretakers who lived there permanently were in their quarters and he'd listened for hours to the echoes of his own footsteps.

He'd tried to imagine the sound of a child's laughter ringing through the big house, but hadn't quite been able to do it. Hadn't really known if he'd *wanted* to do it. But even as he told himself that, he'd realized a part of him was already making room for his child in his life.

Travis shook his head and scowled into his coffee. Adam on the other hand, sat behind his desk, his feet, crossed at the ankle, perched on one corner of it. "What does she want?" he asked quietly.

"She says, nothing."

"Right." Travis blew out a breath.

Jackson walked back across the floor to face both of his brothers. "Look, she just found out I'm the father. I told you she went to that sperm bank and—"

"I can't believe you did that," Adam interrupted.

"Not the point," Jackson told him, refusing to go back over past mistakes. "Barn door open, horse gone."

"He's right," Travis said, standing up to refill his coffee cup from the thermal pot on Adam's desk. "How it happened doesn't matter. What matters is what comes next."

"What do you *want* to happen next?" Adam asked.

Hell if he knew.

He threw his hands in the air and let them fall to his sides again. This was something he was so not prepared to deal with. Something that had never once come up on his radar screen, so to speak. Now that it was there though, he had to step up and make the decision about how to go forward.

Images of Casey and Mia filled his mind. He was a *father.*

What the hell was he supposed to do with that?

"Jackson?"

Coming up out of his thoughts like a drowning man breaching the surface of a deep lake, Jackson looked at Adam and said quietly, "She's my daughter. I won't be kept away from her. Casey's just going to have to deal with that reality. Mia is a *King.* She's going to grow up knowing what that means."

Adam and Travis exchanged glances and nodding, turned back to him.

"Of course she is," Adam said.

"She's family," Travis put in.

"Her mother's not going to like it," Jackson told them.

"You'll have to find a way to work around that."

"I can do that," he said, though inwardly, he admitted that a woman as stubborn as Casey wasn't going to be easy to outmaneuver.

"There's something else to remember here too," Travis put in a moment later. He waited until both of his brothers were looking at him before saying, "You've got Marian to consider, in all this."

"Marian." Jackson whispered her name and shaking his head, realized he hadn't given her a single thought since the night before. But it didn't matter, he decided. He and Marian had a business arrangement. It wasn't as if this were a great love match, after all. He'd tell her what had happened and let her know the engagement would have to be postponed. "She'll understand."

"What makes you think so?" Adam prompted.

"Because she wants this merger. And her father wants this marriage too," Jackson told him. "Having King Jets linked to the Cornice family airfields will be good advertising for them and they know it. Our presence will bring in even more business for them."

"Still not going to make her happy to hear about the baby," Travis said.

"She'll have to deal with it," Jackson declared, unwilling to accept any other outcome. "I'll simply explain that I just found out I have a daughter."

Silence greeted him. Then he repeated the most earth-shattering part of that last sentence. "I have a *daughter.*"

Travis laughed. "I know just how you feel. Strange, isn't it?"

Strange, yes, Jackson thought as he mentally repeated the word *daughter.* A part of him thrilled to it.

Which shook him some. He hadn't planned on this happening. If someone had asked him flat out if he'd wanted to be a father, he would have said no instantly. But now, faced with the reality of Mia, he found himself wanting to know her. Wanting her to know him.

There was a kernel of something inside him that was already taking root, blossoming despite the strange situation he found himself in. There was a little girl alive right now because of him. Didn't that mean that they already had a connection, however slight?

His brothers each looked at him with understanding and he appreciated knowing that he wasn't alone in this. After all, they'd already proven they could survive fatherhood.

"Seems like the King brothers are going to produce all girls in this generation," Travis mused.

"Give me a houseful just like Emma and I'll be happy," Adam said, then frowned. "Until boys start coming around."

"We don't have to worry about that just yet," Travis said.

Jackson though, paled a little. He'd just discovered his daughter, now he had to worry about her growing up? Dating? Meeting guys like *him?*

Being a father just got a lot more complicated.

The following morning, Casey had Mia happily spending time in her walker, bumping around the floor, the plastic wheels making a whirring noise, alerting Casey to her daughter's whereabouts at all times. Mia's throaty laughter spilled into the sunshine-filled room and Casey was smiling as she bent over the graphics program on her computer.

Her home business, *Papyrus,* had really taken off lately. She designed and made exclusive brochures, gift cards, high-end stationery and invitations for every occasion from weddings to birthday parties. She had a small, but select clientele and that list was steadily growing, thanks to word of mouth.

She made her own hours, worked out of her home and had plenty of time to devote to her daughter. The best of all possible worlds. If there was a niggling seed of worry called Jackson King at the back of her mind on this beautiful morning, she made a concerted effort to ignore it.

Talking to Dani the night before had actually reinforced Casey's belief that she wouldn't have to be concerned about Jackson. Yes, Dani thought he'd be back, but Casey was sure her friend was wrong about this. Jackson was simply not the kind of man to be interested in a daughter he'd had no choice in creating. Mia did not fit into his lifestyle, for which Casey was grateful.

No doubt, Jackson was already in one of his luxury jets, flying off to Paris, or London....

"What would that be like?" she whispered, leaning back in her desk chair and staring across the room at Mia, busily chewing the ear of her beloved teddy bear. "Imagine that, sweetie, jumping into your own jet and taking off whenever you felt like it. Where would we go?"

Mia babbled, waved her arms and accidentally tossed Teddy to the ground. Before her little mouth had completely turned down to initiate crying, Casey was up and out of her chair. Picking up the lop-eared toy, she knelt down in front of Mia, handed Teddy back to her and leaned in to plant a kiss on her forehead.

"What do you think, sweetie? London? No," she said as Mia shook her head, laughing. "You're right. London in springtime, way too rainy. Okay, Paris then! We'll go to the Louvre and I'll show you all the beautiful paintings. Would you like that?"

Naturally, Mia didn't understand the question, but she loved having her mom's full attention, so she jumped up and down in her seat and babbled excitedly.

"Good! We'll go on one of those dinner cruises, too, what do you think? We'll see all the pretty lights of the city and get you some yummy French baby food?"

Mia giggled again and Casey paused just to listen. Was there any more wonderful sound than that deep-from-the-belly laugh her daughter had? Mia's big brown eyes sparkled, her wisps of dark brown hair flew about her head in a soft halo and her chubby cheeks were rosy.

"What did I ever do without you?" Casey asked, suddenly filled with so much love, she could hardly stand it. Scooping the baby out of her chair, she cuddled her close, burying her face in the curve of Mia's neck to inhale that soft scent that was so completely Mia.

Pulling back, Casey looked at her little girl and said wistfully, "I should have thanked your daddy. Whether or not he knows it, he gave me the most amazing gift ever."

The doorbell rang and Casey, carrying Mia, walked out of her cramped, makeshift office, down the short hall and through the small, cluttered living room. Evidence of Mia's presence in the house was everywhere. From the playpen tucked beneath the front window to the toys on the floor and the neatly folded clean clothes in the laundry basket perched on the love seat.

Casey shifted Mia higher on her hip and automatically leaned in to look through the peephole in the front door.

Jackson.

He looked different than he had the night before. He was wearing blue jeans today and a black T-shirt that molded itself to his broad chest. On the left breast pocket of the shirt, there was a stylized gold crown with the words

King Jets beneath it. He looked more approachable today and therefore…more dangerous.

Instantly, Casey's heartbeat raced and her mouth went dry. What was he doing here? How did he find her?

"How?" she whispered, answering her own foolish question. "You told him your name and where you lived. Of course he found you. Idiot."

The doorbell rang again and Mia squealed.

"Shh…" Casey winced, and jiggled her daughter, hoping to keep her quiet.

"I can hear the baby," Jackson called through the door.

The timbre of his voice resonated throughout Casey's body. She tried to tell herself that the shivers it created was nothing more than nerves. But even she wasn't buying it. Her body, despite what her mind would have preferred, was reacting to the man exactly as it had the first night they met.

Like a lit match set to dynamite.

"Open the door, Casey," he said, voice just loud enough to carry.

"Why?" she called back, when she knew it was useless to pretend she wasn't home. Her car was in the driveway and Mia was burbling loud enough to alert him.

"I want to talk to you."

"We said everything we had to say last night."

"You might have," he acknowledged, "but I haven't even started yet."

She chanced another look through the peephole and this time, met his stare directly. He'd bent down and was staring right back at her as if he could see her, as well.

Those dark brown eyes were filled with a quiet determination and Casey knew he wouldn't be leaving until she'd heard him out. Her shoulders slumped in defeat before straightening again with a touch of defiance. He wanted to talk? Fine. She'd let him say his piece, then they could go their separate ways.

"Your daddy's awful pushy," she whispered as she flipped the dead bolt lock and slowly opened the door.

"I heard that, too." One of Jackson's dark eyebrows arched as he gave her a cool look just before he stepped past her into the house.

Casey closed the door and locked it, then turned around to look at him. Jackson King standing in the middle of her living room somehow dwarfed her whole house.

True, the older bungalow was tiny anyway, but it had always seemed more than sufficient for her and Mia. Now though, with the strength of Jackson's presence, the house seemed to shrink substantially in size.

His gaze was on hers and she felt the heat of that stare burn right into her. His dark hair was windblown, his jaw was clenched tight and as he folded his arms across his chest and braced his feet wide apart in what looked like a battle stance, she felt a zip of something hot and undeniable.

How could she possibly keep reacting sexually to a man she should be avoiding? And how could she keep him from noticing?

"I didn't expect to see you again," she said, walking past him, and silently cursing the fact that since she had to move sideways to do it, her breasts brushed against his chest. Did he just move in even closer?

"Then that just proves you don't know me as well as you think." His voice was whiskey rough and pitched low enough to send ripples of awareness skittering along Casey's spine.

Darn it.

Determined to at least behave as if she wasn't thrown for a loop by his unannounced visit, Casey headed for an overstuffed chair near Mia's playpen. Once she was seated, she turned Mia around to sit on her lap and looked up at Jackson. He seemed to tower over her. She didn't really remember him being this tall. This intimidating.

Glancing around the room, he spotted a low hassock, gave it a shove with the toe of a scuffed-up cowboy boot and when it was positioned in front of her, he sat down on it. Elbows braced on his knees, he turned the full force of his dark gaze on her and Casey held her breath for a slow count of ten before asking, "Why are you here, Jackson?"

"To talk."

"About?"

"Mia."

She stiffened.

His gaze locked on hers, he said, "I know that neither one of us was expecting this."

She nodded, since her throat was suddenly so tight, she didn't think she'd be able to squeeze out a single word. Did he have to sit so closely? Did he have to smell so good? Did he have to have a voice that sounded like hot nights and silk sheets?

"So," he said, his tone pleasant, though his eyes were dark and unreadable. "Since we find ourselves in a unique position, I've got a unique solution to the situation."

She found her voice. It was scratchy and she was forced to clear her throat, but she managed. "I didn't realize we required a 'solution'."

"Then you were wrong again," he said and gave her a brief half smile.

"Jackson..."

"You've lived here three years, right?"

The statement was so far out of the blue, she only blinked at him for a second or two. "How do you know that?"

"You rent it."

She shifted, lifted her chin and said, "Did you investigate me or something?"

"Why wouldn't I? You show up claiming I'm the father of your child, it only makes sense to check you out."

"I can't believe this." Nerves jumped inside her and Casey suddenly felt as though she couldn't draw enough air into her lungs. She felt trapped in the little house she'd always loved so much.

"Since you rent, it'll make things easier all the way around." He nodded thoughtfully, glanced at the cramped quarters and she could guess exactly what he was thinking. He came from big, towering piles of money. He owned a mansion he rarely used and kept hotel suites ready "just in case." He had no idea what life for real people was like and she was sure he was mentally dismissing the home she'd made for Mia and herself.

But Casey had nothing to be ashamed of. The house was small, but it was clean and cute and just enough for her and her daughter. And if he had investigated her background, then he knew she was honest, paid her bills on time and that she was completely capable of caring for *her* child.

He could think whatever he liked. It really didn't matter to her one way or the other.

"That will make this easier," he said at last.

"Make *what* easier?"

"I want you and Mia to move in with me."

Five

"You're crazy!"

"Possibly. You know, it's the oddest thing," Jackson mused as he watched her features register complete and total shock. "Your eyes change color according to your moods."

She shook her head as if she couldn't believe she'd heard him correctly. "What?"

He'd done that on purpose. Put her off guard. Off balance. Never sure what he'd do next. Besides, her eyes did intrigue him. But then, *she* intrigued him. More than he was comfortable admitting.

"Your eyes," he said. "They seem a very pale blue usually. But when you're mad—like now—or when I'm inside you…" he paused and watched his words hit home, "that soft blue becomes as dark and deep as the ocean."

She squirmed uneasily in her chair. Good. She should be uneasy. He was. Damn it, she'd thrown him for a hard loop since the moment he'd first spotted her at the hotel bar. Seemed only fair he return the favor.

Since meeting with his brothers the day before, Jackson had been in high gear. One thing you could say for the Kings, they knew how to get things done fast.

He'd placed a single phone call to the King family attorneys and within a few hours, he'd not only gained several new employees at his home and every stick of furniture an infant required, but he'd known everything about Casey Davis that there was to know. He wasn't sure how the law firm had managed it, but he assumed they had people on the payroll who could pull off minor miracles when necessary.

Even knowing that he'd come here to draw a line in the sand, all Jackson could think now was, he wanted to touch Casey again. Feel her eager response, the sigh of her breath on his neck. Drown in the heat of her body.

He shook his head, dislodging the erotic images that flooded his mind, so that he could concentrate on the problem at hand.

"You can't be serious about us moving in with you." Her arms tightened around Mia until the baby squirmed uncomfortably in her mother's grasp.

He'd expected just such a reaction. And if he were to be honest with himself, it was a crazy idea. He was supposed to be on the verge of getting engaged. Marrying a woman who was completely unaware of Mia and Casey's existence. And truth be told, he hadn't come here with the idea of moving the two of them into his house. He'd come to demand time with his daughter. But one look at the tiny rental on the ragged edge of town where his daughter lived had convinced him that she deserved better.

And she'd get it.

As for Marian, he'd talk to her. Explain that he needed more time. He couldn't go into a marriage—not even one that was a strictly business proposition—until he had the rest of his life straightened out.

And who would have thought it would need straightening? He'd always lived his life as he chose. Making his own decisions. Never factoring in anyone else's opinion.

Seemed those days were over.

"There's plenty of room. I've got a nursery completely outfitted already and plenty of help in the house for you if you need it."

"I don't."

"So you've said. Repeatedly." He shifted on the footstool and the old leather creaked with the movement. "But I've been doing a lot of thinking about this."

"And *this* is your plan?"

"That's right." He got up from the too-low footstool, not because his long legs were cramped but because he was too close to Casey. Her scent reached for him. The curve of her breasts tempted him and her mouth all but begged to be kissed.

And that wasn't why he was here. This wasn't about him and Casey. This was about his daughter.

He walked two short paces—all he could take without actually leaving the room—stopped beside the playpen and idly rested one hand on the rim. "Look, I might never have planned on being a father, but I am one now and that changes things."

Her chin lifted, her eyes narrowed and her grip on Mia tightened as if she were half afraid he was going to grab the baby and make a run for it. "I don't see how."

He laughed shortly. "Of course you don't."

She took a breath, blew it out and said, "I know what you're doing…."

"Is that right?" He let go of the playpen, folded his arms over his chest and looked down at her.

"Men like you—"

"Like me?"

"The take-charge type," she explained.

"Ah."

"Men like you see a situation and immediately jump in and start shifting things around. For some reason, you've decided that Mia and I are *your* business. We're not."

"We disagree," he said, his gaze slipping from her now dark blue eyes to the baby on her lap and back again.

She blew out a frustrated breath. "I don't know how to say this so you'll understand me. You don't owe us anything. I don't want your money and I don't need your help."

Well, that stung. True or not. And it was clearly, he thought with another rueful glance around her tiny, cluttered home, not true.

"Let's cut to the bottom line here, shall we?" he asked tightly.

Casey stood up and he silently admired the move. She wasn't content to sit there having to look up at him. Instead, she'd taken action to put them on more equal footing. Or so she thought. Her yellow T-shirt was hiked up beneath Mia's chubby leg, but her eyes were steady and her features were schooled into a carefully stoic mask. "Let's."

"I don't want my daughter living here."

She sucked in a breath as if he'd slapped her. "There's nothing wrong with our house."

"Not the best neighborhood," he said.

"We're perfectly safe."

"My daughter deserves better."

"*My* daughter is happy here."

Jackson knew this little verbal battle could go on for hours, so he decided to end it. Moving in close to her, he looked down into her eyes, inhaled the scent of lavender that clung to her and said, "We can do this one of two ways. A, you and Mia move in with me for say, six months. I get to know my daughter and at the end of that time, I'll buy you a house anywhere you want."

"I don't—"

"Or B," he said loudly, to drown out her voice and force her to listen to his counterproposal. "You insist on staying here and I make a phone call to the family lawyers. Within a couple of hours, you'll be notified that I'm suing for joint custody. And if you think I can't…remember, you contacted me. You broke the anonymity clause."

Her eyes went wild and wide. Like a trapped animal looking desperately for a way out of a dangerous situation. But there was no way out and Jackson knew it. He had her boxed in neatly.

"You…why would…"

"I'm not the bad guy here," he said.

"Could have fooled me," she muttered.

"Let's remember here that I only just found out about Mia's existence. I want to know my child. Is that really so unreasonable to you?"

"No, but expecting us to change everything about our lives, is."

"You have a choice."

"Some choice." Shaking her head, she stared up at him and the sheen of tears in her eyes threw him for a second. He hoped to hell she didn't cry. He hated it when women cried. He always felt helpless—not a feeling he was comfortable with.

"You're a bully," she whispered, willing the tears back.

"Excuse me?"

"You heard me. You're a bully. You're rich and powerful and think you can just sweep in and get anything you want."

He thought about that for a long minute, letting his gaze sweep up and down her curvy body. Finally, he said, "When I want something bad enough, yes."

She pulled in a deep breath and held the baby even closer than before. Then lifting her chin, Casey said, "Fine then. You win this one. We'll move into your house for six months. You'll get to know your daughter and then we'll leave."

"Wise choice."

"But just so you know," she said, "your tactics won't work on everything. You can't have *me*. What happened between us that first night? It's not going to be happening again. Do you understand?"

Jackson's body was hard and ready and he wanted her even more now than he had when he'd first walked through her front door. He shouldn't though and he'd do his damnedest to ignore the rush of desire that jumped through him whenever he laid eyes on her. Because he had plans for his life. And they didn't include Casey Davis, no matter how alluring she might be.

So he smiled and met her gaze as he said, "None of this is about you, Casey. This is about my daughter."

Movers arrived the following Saturday. Casey sat in a lawn chair on the front yard beside Dani, the two of them watching the kids roll around on a quilt spread beneath the jacaranda tree. A three-year-old boy and two baby girls were surprisingly loud.

"I know you don't want to hear this," Dani said as they watched two movers carry boxes out of the house, "but Mike's glad you're moving."

"What?" Casey looked at her, then reached down and pulled a stick from Mia's grip. "I thought your husband liked me."

"He does, you nut," Dani said. "But he's also a cop. And he says this neighborhood isn't a good one for a single woman and a baby."

Casey frowned. Okay, it wasn't a ritzy area, but the houses were mostly tidy and the teenagers weren't too annoying and she'd only had graffiti spray-painted on her garage the one time.

"He never said anything…."

"He didn't want you to be scared or anything," Dani

said, instantly defending the husband she was so crazy about. "But he always cruises your neighborhood at night, keeping an eye on things."

Casey sighed. That sounded like Mike. Such a nice man. Unlike some others she could name. Mike didn't push his views on her, try to run her life. He just quietly did what he could to keep her safe.

Why couldn't Jackson be more like that?

"So I'm not surprised your Jackson wanted you to move."

"He's not *my* Jackson, for heaven's sake," Casey said quickly and scowled as her insides did a quick ripple of expectation at the sound of his name. "And he's not interested in my safety, believe me. He just wants Mia."

"She is his daughter."

Casey shot her a dark look. "Traitor."

Dani laughed and scooped her baby girl up into her lap to pull a leaf out of her mouth. "I'm just saying there are worse things in life than to be scooped up by a gorgeous millionaire and whisked off to his hilltop mansion."

Sure, when you said it like that, Casey thought, it was like something out of a romantic movie. Almost Cinderella-like. Poor but honest girl meets rich handsome prince and finds love and happily ever after. But Casey knew the truth. The only thing between her and Jackson—except for some incredible heat—was Mia.

He wasn't a prince. At the moment, she thought of him more like a cartoon villain, evilly twirling his moustache.

"He threatened to take Mia."

Dani sighed. "If he'd actually meant to do that, he could have. He's probably got a fleet of lawyers on standby.

Instead, he just wants to get to know his kid. You really can't blame him for that."

"Why not?" When Dani only looked at her, Casey laughed. "Okay, I know. I'm overreacting."

"Just a bit," Dani agreed. "I mean, I get why, but you'd probably have been furious if Mia's father had turned out to be some miserable creep who wanted nothing to do with her, too."

"Maybe…" The truth was, she could understand Jackson's interest in his daughter. That didn't mean she had to like it, though.

"Casey, try not to treat this move as if it's a jail sentence. Look at it like a minivacation."

"A vacation?"

"Sure. He's got a huge place. Plenty of room for you to work and Mia to play. There'll be someone else for you to lean on once in awhile. You won't have to do it all yourself…."

She liked doing everything herself. She was used to it. She'd made her way, built a business, was raising a beautiful child. Why should she look for help she didn't need?

Besides, "Can you really see Jackson King changing diapers?"

Dani shrugged. "Guess you'll find out. But the point is, stop sabotaging this before it starts."

Was she? Or was Dani seeing only a silver lining and disregarding the huge, massive black cloud currently sitting over Casey's head? Case in point…the movers. They were carrying Mia's crib now and the rocking chair that Casey had painted herself.

"Um, didn't you say Jackson told you he outfitted a nursery?"

"Yes," Casey said tightly. Only the best for the daughter of a King. "He arranged to put my stuff in storage for six months." Without bothering to ask her. He'd just called her with the information and when she'd tried to argue that she wanted to take her stuff with her to his house, he'd simply steamrolled right over her.

"Ah…"

A cool wind kicked up, scattering twigs and lacy leaves across the lawn. Casey shivered a little. Was she making a huge mistake? Should she have stood up to Jackson? Gone to court rather than caving to his demands? She looked down at Mia and a small thread of fear wrapped itself around her heart.

"I can do this, right?"

"Of course you can."

"It'll be good for Mia."

"Positively."

Oh, God. "Is it too late to run away?" Casey wondered aloud.

"It is if that's Prince Charming in your carriage," Dani told her, pointing to a big black SUV pulling up in front of the house.

Casey didn't have to see the driver to know it was Jackson. She could tell because her body had started humming and her stomach was doing somersaults. Six months of living in his house? Being around him night and day? How was she going to manage this?

Before she could come up with an answer to that question,

Jackson opened the door and stepped out of the car. Beside her, Dani sighed heavily. Not hard to understand. Jackson was wearing black slacks, a long-sleeved white shirt with the sleeves rolled back on his tanned, muscled forearms and sunglasses that he slipped off as he walked toward them. Prince Charming? Maybe. Dangerous? Absolutely.

"Remember," her friend said, "you're going to make this work."

Casey's mouth was dry, just watching him walk across the lawn, so she nodded.

"Casey," he said, smiling. His gaze dropped briefly to Mia and even Casey saw his dark eyes warm.

"Hello, Jackson," she said when she found her voice again. "You didn't have to come by, I was going to drive to your place later."

"Not necessary," he said, turning a smile on Dani. Casey didn't even have to see her friend's face to know she was being sucked into Jackson's orbit. The man was definitely high on the charisma chart when he wanted to be.

"Jackson King," he said, holding out one hand.

"Dani Sullivan." She shook his hand, turned to Casey and lifted both eyebrows.

Casey ignored her and did her best to rise above the charm level Jackson was using. "I can't go with you and leave my car here."

"Don't worry about it. One of my guys will drive it over to the house later."

"Your guys?"

"Employees," Jackson corrected for her benefit.

"Besides, your little compact's not the safest car in the world to haul a baby around in."

Casey was stunned. "Of course it's safe. I take it in for checkups regularly."

"Not what I mean," he said, waving one hand at the pale-blue compact parked on one side of her driveway. "Look at it. In an accident, you might as well be riding a skateboard."

Dani winced and Casey stared at him. "I don't get in accidents."

"Not purposely," he conceded. "But then that's why they're called 'accidents'."

"He's got you there," Dani muttered.

Casey scowled at her friend, then shifted that same expression to Jackson. "My car is perfectly serviceable."

"Uh-huh, maybe it used to be." He turned, pointed to the black monster parked at the curb, then looked back at Casey. "*That's* your car, now."

"I—my—what?"

"I bought you a car," he said, in the same tone he might have used when saying, *I made you a sandwich.* "Had the dealer install a top-of-the-line car seat for Mia, so you're all set there, too. Much safer for you and the baby."

Casey wasn't an idiot. She could see that he was most likely right about that monstrous car/bus being safer to ride in. After all, it looked the size of a small tank. But she couldn't keep allowing him to ride roughshod on her life anymore. A line had to be drawn. Might as well be done now.

"Jackson, you can't go around doing things like that," she said, staring at the car now and trying to imagine herself behind the wheel. It was so huge it would be like driving an eighteen-wheeler. And the thought of how much it would cost simply to fill the gas tank gave her a sinking sensation in the pit of her stomach.

"Why not? You needed a safer car, I got it for you."

He really didn't get it. Didn't seem to understand that she wasn't the kind of woman to be taken over by some big strong male who thought he knew what was best for her. For heaven's sake, she was an adult. She'd been making her own way and her own decisions for most of her life.

Now, all because she'd felt it was his right to know about Mia's existence, her life was wildly spinning out of control. That old saying about *good deeds never going unpunished,* was certainly true enough.

But that ship had sailed and there was no going back. Dani was right, she'd have been furious if Mia's father hadn't wanted to know her, too. So there really had been no win to this situation and the fact that Jackson was clearly determined to be a part of his daughter's life said *something* about his character.

And even if she didn't like it, having a father would be good for Mia. That's what she had to keep in mind, here. What was best for Mia.

Still, she had to make him see that while he might be related to Mia, he had no control over Casey. So she tried again, speaking slowly and plainly. "I don't need a new—"

"It's in your name. Temporary registration and insurance information are in the glove compartment. Why don't you drive it on our trip back to my place, get used to the feel of it?" He smiled and started for the house. "I'll just check with the movers, make sure they know where to take your stuff."

"I already told them—" Her voice trailed off as Jackson walked away, clearly not trusting her to have been able to instruct movers. "Did you see that?"

"Deep breath," Dani said, putting one hand on Casey's forearm. "Okay, I see what you mean. He is a little—"

"Overbearing? Bossy?"

"Yeah." Dani gave her a pat of reassurance. "He is. But it seems like he means well."

"He's impossible."

"Honey, it's only six months."

"Six months," she repeated and thought that very shortly, she would be using those two words as a mantra.

Casey turned to look at the little house that had been hers. Where she and Mia had built so many memories. She knew she was looking at her past, because no matter what happened over the next six months, she and her daughter wouldn't return to this place. And nothing would be the same, ever again.

Jackson stepped out of the house, walked to the edge of the porch and looked at her. Across the yard, despite the presence of the movers, Dani, and the kids, Casey felt the power of his steady gaze reach out to her. Even from this distance, even surrounded by people, she felt heat building inside her. Just a look from him gave her shivers. Her body didn't seem to care that he was the human embodiment of a bulldozer. Didn't care that he was taking over her life.

All her body wanted, was *his* body.

Six

Through the baby monitor, Casey heard Mia whimpering in her sleep. Slipping out of her wide, sumptuous bed, Casey grabbed up her terry-cloth robe and headed for the door of her room.

It wasn't surprising that Mia was awake and fretful. Their day had been filled with strange people, strange places. Even Casey was finding it hard to sleep in a new place. No wonder then that the baby was feeling just as unsettled.

Skylights dotted the roof over the long hallway, letting in moonlight that guided her way along the corridor to the room beside hers. While she hurried to Mia, Casey's mind raced.

Jackson had naturally stepped in and taken over moving day. When they arrived at his sprawling hilltop home, Casey had been amazed to see just how much the man had accomplished in one week. Not only was her bedroom the most elegant, luxurious room she'd ever set foot in, but Mia's nursery was the sort she was used to seeing in celebrity magazine articles.

There was a mural of forest animals on the walls, a closet stuffed with clothing, shelves filled with toys and a crib fit for a princess. The lower half of the windows in the second story nursery were barred for safety's sake and looked out over the sweeping landscape that rushed downhill toward the ocean.

Casey, on her own, never could have provided her daughter with anything like the well-appointed room. And though she appreciated all Jackson had done to make their daughter a space in his life, she couldn't help feeling the sharp sting of envy.

He was using his money to point out the differences in their lives and he was doing a good job of it.

She reached Mia's room and the door was partially open, as she'd insisted it remain earlier. The baby's cries had stopped on Casey's short walk down the hall, but she had kept going, wanting to reassure herself that Mia was safely back to sleep. Now, Casey heard whispers just carrying over the baby's sniffling breaths.

Curious, Casey pushed the door open silently, and paused on the threshold. Moonlight flooded this room as well, and the night-light that had been left burning was a magical thing that threw patches of stars onto the ceiling.

But she hardly noticed any of it. Instead, her gaze focused on the man standing beside the crib, holding Mia against his chest.

"No more tears, Mia," he murmured and his already

deep voice was a rumble of hushed sound. "You're safe here. This is your new home…."

Casey's heart twisted as she watched him soothing their daughter. Clearly, he'd left his own bed to come to this room. He wore silk pajama bottoms that hung low on his narrow hips and the chest he held his daughter against was bare and gleamed like carved bronze in the moonlight. His dark head was bent toward Mia's and Casey heard his soft whispers as he soothed the tiny girl he held so carefully.

"Go back to sleep, baby girl," he said on a soft sigh. "Dream of rainbows and puppies and long summer days. Your daddy's here now and nothing will ever hurt you…."

She couldn't tear her gaze from them. There was something so sweet, so…right about the picture they made. Calling himself Mia's daddy, promising that sweet little girl that she'd never be hurt, all of it made Casey want to both smile and cry.

Jackson swayed gently, continuing the quiet rush of whispers and Mia's tiny sigh sounded gently in the room. And Casey's tears won the battle, stinging her eyes, blurring her vision until she had to fight to hold them back.

As if sensing her presence, he turned, still cradling Mia, and smiled at her. "I've got a monitor in my room, too."

Casey walked close to them and reached out one hand to smooth her sleeping baby's hair. "Of course you do."

His eyes narrowed a bit. "I am her father."

"You're right," she said, meeting his dark gaze. "I'm just used to being the only one getting up in the middle of the night."

The look in his eyes gentled some at that admission. His hand moved up and down Mia's back, soothing, stroking. "I can understand that," he whispered. "But you're not alone anymore, Casey. I'm here. And I'm going to be a part of Mia's life. I've already missed too much."

She took a deep breath and nodded. This was only their first night together. She was going to have to find a way to deal with Jackson's rights as a father.

Forcing a smile, she said, "You seem handier with babies than I expected."

Apparently realizing that she was willing to if not end their little war, then to at least declare a temporary cease-fire, Jackson smiled. "I've got two nieces, remember? Emma and Katie. Emma's a little more than a year old and Katie's about three months. I've put in my babysitting time."

Her surprise must have been stamped on her features because his smile widened into a grin that made her catch her breath.

"Didn't know that, did you?" he asked.

"No. I mean," she said, "I knew about your brothers' children, I just never thought you would—"

"What?" he challenged. "Love my family?"

Well, that made her feel small and petty. She should have known better. Should have guessed. In the research she'd done on Jackson before meeting him in person, she'd learned just how tight the King family really was. She just hadn't even thought that a man more interested in jetting off to exotic places would be so attentive to his infant nieces.

"Of course not," she said softly as Jackson turned and expertly laid a sleeping Mia back in her crib, "I just didn't think a man like you would want anything to do with babies."

"A man like me?"

She moved past him, bent over the top rail of the beautiful white crib and ran the flat of her hand down Mia's back. Listening to her child's quiet snuffles and sighs, she smiled. "You know," she said as she turned back to him. "The playboy type."

He laughed quietly. "You think I'm a playboy?"

She turned her head to look at him and almost wished she hadn't. While he'd been holding Mia, he was gorgeous, but somehow safe. Now that he wasn't…he looked much too tempting. All that bare, tanned, muscled flesh. The sleep-ruffled hair. The shadow of whiskers on his jaw. The heavy-lidded sexiness of his eyes.

Oh, God.

"I only know what I read about you," she said and moved for the door. Best to get back to her own room fast, before she did something really stupid like reaching out one hand to trace the planes of those muscles of his.

He was just a step behind her and when they moved into the hall, he caught her arm. Heat shot from his touch to rocket through her body like an explosion battering off a series of walls. She was forced to lock her knees to keep from swaying into him. His eyes were dark, fathomless and when he spoke, she had to fight for focus.

"And just what have you read?"

"I think you know the answer to that," she said, trying to tug her arm free of his grasp. "You're practically the poster boy for fast jets and faster women. So you can understand how seeing you, being so gentle, so tender, with Mia like that, could throw me a little."

He snorted. "You've got a narrow view on the world, don't you?"

"No, I don't." She tried again to get free, but Jackson wasn't ready to let her go just yet. He parted her robe and ran one hand up her arm. Even though the terry robe she wore wasn't exactly sexy, seeing the curve of her breasts beneath the soft fabric was enough to make him hard and ready and way too eager. Despite the fact that she had the ability to seriously annoy him.

"Sure you do," he said with a sneer. "You read some one-sided articles about me and decide that I'm what? Some rampaging guy, only interested in what he can take out of life?"

She stilled and chewed on her bottom lip. He'd like to help with that, but he resisted.

"Do you think the tabloids would be interested in doing a story on me babysitting my nieces? No," he answered for her. "They want sensationalism because that's what people like you want to read."

Her eyes, a dark, passion-filled blue, widened. "People like me?"

"Not fun being judged, is it?" he countered. "Yes, people like you. People who see a headline about me on a grocery store paper and assume you know me." He bent down, until their gazes were on the same level and his mouth was just a breath away from hers. "I'm not that guy, Casey. There's more to me than that, just as I assume there's more to you than the woman who seduced me just to get a DNA sample."

She tried to pull away again, but wasn't successful. Jackson stared down into her eyes and felt the tug of the attraction between them arc like a downed power line, sparks flying, hissing, through the air.

He'd leapt out of bed when he'd heard Mia crying. Hadn't stopped to consider that he'd no doubt run into Casey along the way.

It had been instinct drawing him to his crying child. Instinct to lift her from the crib and a revelation when those tiny arms had come around his neck. Love like he'd never known had dropped down on him like a thunderbolt from the sky.

Feeling the solid weight of his daughter in his arms, the slide of her tears over his skin and her tiny fingers pulling at his hair, Jackson had taken the fall. Her helplessness, her vulnerability had come together to catch him in a silken trap and hold him fast.

There was no escape for him, ever. Not even if he'd wanted one, which he didn't. He was his daughter's father and he would fight anyone who tried to keep them apart. Even if it meant going to war with her mother.

But looking down at Casey now, he knew damn well he didn't want to fight her. What he wanted was to pick her up, carry her into his room and bury himself inside her. He hungered for her touch. For the feel of her skin beneath his hands. He wanted her so badly, the need clawed at his throat, nearly choking him.

A small voice inside reminded him that he was soon

supposed to be an engaged man. But he wasn't there yet. No promises had been made, so none could be broken.

And that's when a new plan hit him. He'd told Casey that he wasn't interested in her. A lie, of course, but one that had suited him at the time. But she and Mia were here in his house, now. And that changed things. Rather than a war, Jackson decided he'd wage a different kind of battle. A battle of seduction.

The amazing chemistry between them was too hot for either of them to pretend it didn't exist. So maybe, if they surrendered to it, they could burn out the flame faster than they could by ignoring it.

He backed her against the wall and watched her eyes widen even further. The pulse point at the base of her throat pounded and her breath quickened until her breasts lifted and fell in rapid succession. She felt everything he did. He saw it in her eyes.

"Jackson, don't," she whispered, looking up into his eyes. "Like you said, we don't even know each other."

"That didn't stop us the night we met."

"That was different," she murmured even as he covered one of her breasts with his palm. His thumb slowly stroked across the tip of her hardened nipple.

She gasped and he knew it was from both desire and shock. She hadn't expected him to make a move on her and damned if he didn't like having the element of surprise on his side. And the feel of her. Even through the soft cloth of her robe, the heat of her swept into his palm, feeding the fires within until he felt as if he might spontaneously combust on the spot.

"Not really," he whispered, and kissed her briefly, gently, a featherlight touch of his lips to hers. "Besides, what better way to get to know each other?"

"It would be a mistake," she said, even as she arched into his hand.

"Are you so sure," he murmured, dropping his other hand to the hem of her robe, lifting it, sliding it up her thigh, letting his fingertips trail across her silky skin.

"Um…" She closed her eyes, moaned a little and then sighed as his fingers toyed with her nipple. "Yes?"

He smiled and shifted his hand higher on her leg, sliding inexorably toward the heart of her. The heated, silken core of her body. He needed to touch. To stroke. "You don't sound very sure to me, but then maybe I don't know you well enough to be certain."

"Exactly," she whispered, her eyes flying open again to meet his.

"Help me then," he said as he discovered she wasn't wearing panties. He stroked her heat and watched her eyes darken even further until that midnight blue looked nearly black. "What's your favorite color?"

"What?" Startled, she shook her head, whimpered and parted her legs a bit to give him easier access. "Color?"

"Your favorite," he prodded.

"Blue. Yours?"

"Black. Mountains or beach?"

"Beach. You?"

"Mountains," he whispered and slid one finger into her heat. She sighed and he asked, "Picnic or restaurant?"

"Picnic."

"Restaurant." Two fingers now, dipping in and out of her heat, sliding, pushing, stroking. Her eyes wheeled, and she bit down on her bottom lip to keep her moans of pleasure stifled. "Paris or Rome?"

She shook her head against the wall. "Never seen either." Her breath came in shattered gasps. "But Paris, I think."

"I'll take you to Rome," he promised, "you'll like it better, trust me." He watched as pleasure etched itself into her features. He felt the tension in her climb, sensed how near she was to climax and pushed her closer. His thumb stroked the most sensitive bud of flesh at the apex of her thighs as his fingers continued their ministrations.

She quivered, held onto his shoulders and dug her fingers into his bare skin. She rocked her hips into his hand, moving fretfully, anxiously, chasing the release she knew was just out of reach.

"Now we know each other," he whispered, his mouth aligned with hers. He looked into her eyes, willed her to give herself to him.

"And we have nothing in common," she told him.

"Do you care?" He touched her deeper, harder.

She groaned. "No."

"Me neither," he said. "No more excuses. So come for me. Let me watch you fall."

"I can't," she said between harsh breaths, her hips moving, her head moving from side to side. "It's too much. I can't just—"

"Let go," he demanded, his own hunger crashing through him. Gazes locked, Jackson felt her surrender and a moment later, watched as she splintered. He swallowed her moan with his mouth, taking her soft sighs and puffs of breath as his own. He felt her body contract around his fingers and continued to stroke her long after the last ripple had faded away.

Reluctant to release her, he finally picked her up, considered taking her back to her room and finally decided on his own. There at least, were condoms in the side table drawer. A few long steps and he was there. He carried her inside, kicking the door shut behind them. In his arms, her eyes were still glazed and her mouth was open, an invitation to a kiss.

He accepted and took her lips with his as he walked across his darkened room, following a swatch of moonlight that speared in through the wide bank of windows. Setting her down on the edge of the wide mattress, he wasted no time in grasping her robe and whipping it off of her, baring her body to his gaze. In the pale wash of light, her skin looked like the finest porcelain. Her nipples were hardened tips of pale pink and the thatch of dark blond curls at the apex of her thighs tempted him.

"Jackson—" Even as she sat there, naked, he could see her mind working, providing reason after reason as to why this was a bad idea. Giving her plenty of excuses to call this off. To stop him before it was too late.

"No thinking tonight," he said, shutting her down before she could get started. "Just feeling. We're in this together, Casey. Let's enjoy it."

She laughed shortly and shook her head. "This isn't why I came here. This isn't what was supposed to happen."

"This was *destined* to happen," he argued, loosening the

ties of his pajama bottoms and letting them fall to the floor.

She sucked in a breath.

"We both know it," he said. "We've known it all along."

Her gaze drifted over him and his already hard body tightened further. When she looked up, into his eyes, he reminded her, "From that first night, Casey, we were meant for this. Tell me you know it. You feel it."

"I don't know," she admitted, shaking her head, licking her lips. "I don't know what I feel anymore."

"Let me help." He set one knee on the mattress and pressed her back onto the bed. She stared up at him in the moonlight and Jackson felt a surging roar of need rise within. She touched something in him, made him crave like he'd never done before. She reached him in places no other woman had and though he didn't want to take the time to explore those feelings, he definitely wanted to enjoy them.

He wanted her over, under and around him. He wanted her legs locked over his hips. He wanted her on top, taking him inside her heat. He wanted to watch her eyes flash with climax. Wanted to hear her soft moans and desperate sighs. And he wasn't willing to wait another moment for any of it.

Reaching to one side, he yanked open the bedside table drawer, pulled out a condom and ripped the foil covering off. Then he sheathed himself, shifted until he was standing between her legs looking down at her and then he smiled.

"Jackson—"

"You want this as much as I do, I know it. And so do you."

She laughed, a tight groan of sound sliding from her

throat as he scooped his hands beneath her behind and lifted. "You're like a force of nature. You show up and take over. You're even convinced you know what I want sexually."

He quirked a brow at her. "You're saying I'm wrong?" He positioned her legs around his hips and held her there until she'd locked her ankles at the small of his back.

"Would it matter?"

"Yes," he said tightly, his fingers exploring her soft folds, caressing, dipping into her heat. "If you tell me to stop, I will."

She hissed in a breath and lifted her hips even higher into his touch. "Don't stop."

"I knew you'd say that."

"Have all the answers, do you?"

"Yeah." The tip of his penis rested at her entrance. Everything in him urged him to plunge. To take. To ravish. To pleasure. And yet he waited. "I told you before, when I know what I want, I find a way to get it."

She whimpered a little, scooted closer, claiming the very tip of him. "And when you're finished taking charge, will you tell me when I've climaxed?"

He laughed and pushed himself into her heat. "You'll know, Casey. Trust me, you'll know."

Her legs tightened around his hips and he rocked into her. Heat devoured him, sensation enveloped him. She fisted her hands in the black silk sheets and held on as he moved in her over and over again, driving them both to the edge of madness, keeping them both teetering on the very brink of release.

Each time he felt her orgasm near, he pulled her back,

deprived her of what she wanted, needed. He prolonged the pleasure for each of them, making each stroke a divine kind of torture.

He'd never known this all-encompassing wash of pleasure. He'd never felt so connected to a woman in his bed. He'd never watched her pleasure and felt it magnify his own. For a man who liked to be in charge of everything in his life, Jackson was suddenly sure that it was Casey driving this train.

Casey, whose soft groans and frantic whispers fed the fires inside him until they burned brighter than he would have thought possible. This was more than he'd found in that first night with her. This was deeper, bigger. This was *more*. Of everything. He felt her desire and stoked it. Felt her tension and created more. He wanted to be the one to take her higher and faster than any other man had before. He wanted to touch her as she had somehow touched him.

When finally, her body fisted around his, Jackson knew he couldn't delay his own release a moment longer. He surrendered to the inevitable. Gave himself up to the woman who had so completely splintered his defenses.

And when the storm passed, he stretched out on the bed beside her, gathered her close and listened to the furious beat of her heart.

Tomorrow would be time enough to figure out what the hell had just happened.

Seven

Over the next week, Jackson alternately buried himself in work and indulged himself at home. But for the first time in his life, he couldn't seem to keep his mind on business and that was a little disconcerting. It was taking all of his focus to maintain schedules, look at new routes and assign his pilots.

Before Casey, he'd spent nearly every waking moment at the airfield. Hanging with the other pilots, taking the jets up, plotting and planning the expansion of King Jets had been his be-all and end-all.

Now, everything had changed.

"I'll take the Vegas run today," Dan Stone said, leaning across Jackson's desk to point to one of the scheduled flights on their weekly roster. "And I can do Phoenix tomorrow," he added, then straightened up. "But you've got to put one of the other guys on the Maine flight Thursday."

"Why?" Jackson looked up at one of his best pilots. Most of King Jets clients were wealthy, pampered and knew what they wanted. They even had favorite pilots and Dan was one that was most often requested.

Jackson acknowledged that for some people, flying was a terrifying ordeal. He just found it hard to understand anyone who didn't love being up in the air, surrounded by clouds, with the ground no more than a smudge of green beneath you. For him, flying was about freedom. Always had been. Dan Stone was just like Jackson in that way, so the fact that the man was turning down a long flight in favor of a couple of short hops was curious.

"It's Patti," Dan said, tucking his hands into the pockets of his black slacks. "She's due any day now and she doesn't want me gone for long."

"Ah." That's right. Jackson had forgotten all about Dan's wife being pregnant with their first child. "Okay then, we'll hand off the Maine flight to Paul Hannah. He should be fine with it. Then once Patti's delivered, you can—"

"That's the thing, boss," Dan interrupted him with a wince. "Patti's a little crazed right now, talking about how she wants me to quit flying. Too dangerous."

"You're kidding." Jackson leaned back in his chair and stared up at the other man. Dan looked uncomfortable as hell.

"Wish I was," the man said with a shake of his head. He walked over to the bank of windows in Jackson's office and looked down at the airfield where blue King Jets were lined up like a military unit on parade. "She's never liked me flying. In fact, it's the one thing that almost kept her from marrying me. She's scared every time I go up. And now that we've got the baby coming…"

Jackson watched his friend. They'd been flying together for years. And he knew that Dan, more than anyone else, understood that soul-deep need Jackson had always had to be in the air. "Can you do it?" he asked. "Quit, I mean. Could you really walk away from flying?"

Dan turned his head and gave Jackson a rueful smile. "I don't know. Never considered such a thing before." He tipped his head so that he could stare up at the blue, cloud-studded sky and a sigh left him. "I do know that Patti and the baby mean more to me than anything—including flying."

Funny, but Jackson had never really thought about the inherent dangers in air travel. To him, being in a plane, behind the controls of a powerful jet, skimming through the sky—it was second nature. Something that was as much a part of him as his brown eyes. Sure, there was a risk whenever you took a plane up. But hell, he faced a higher chance of an accident just taking his car on the freeway.

And he wondered if he could walk away from something he loved so much for the sake of someone he loved more. The question had never come up for him before. Was it because the thought of crashing, dying had never bothered him much since he'd never had anything to lose? As that question resonated in his thoughts, his mind dredged up images of Mia. And Casey.

Casey?

Jackson shifted uneasily in his chair. Loving his daughter was one thing. It was to be expected. But feelings for her mother weren't a part of his game plan. Yes, he wanted her. More every damn day, despite how many times a night they came together. But anything more than lust was simply not allowed to happen. There were other considerations—*Marian.*

That name shot through his mind like a blazing comet, leaving behind a streak of fiery red sparks. Hell, he'd forgotten all about Marian over the last couple of weeks. He'd never called her back after walking out on their dinner together. He'd never bothered to check in to say he'd been busy and he *still* hadn't proposed.

"Everything okay?" Dan asked, frowning at him. "You suddenly look like you've got food poisoning or something."

Not surprising, given the thoughts rushing through his mind. But Jackson shook his head and said, "No, I'm…fine. Just have a lot on my mind."

"I know the feeling," Dan mused with a shrug. "Anyway, I've got some time still to think about this."

"Sure you do," Jackson said, preferring to think about Dan's problems than his own. "And, if you do decide to hang up your wings, I want you to know you've still got a job here." He stood up, held out his hand. "You can take charge of the ground crew, or you can move into design. You've always had a good eye and I can use a man who knows what passengers want in a plane and can look at the designs with a pilot's eye."

Dan nodded, shook Jackson's hand and said, "Thanks, boss. I appreciate it."

When the other man left, Jackson dropped back into his chair. He had to make a call. Had to go see Marian, explain about Mia and tell her they wouldn't be getting married anytime soon.

She wasn't going to be happy about it, but damned if he could bring himself to care. The truth was, it didn't really matter how Marian took the news. The very fact that he hadn't given her a single thought in two weeks told him all he needed to know. Whether the idea to marry into the Cornice family had started as a good one or not, it clearly was a bad idea at the moment.

"I've got news on your Cassiopeia."

"Huh? What?" He glanced up from his desk to find Anna standing in the open doorway of his office. Pushing thoughts of his soon to be ex-almost-fiancée out of his mind, he repeated, "What?"

"Casey? You remember. The girl with blue eyes? The woman you wanted me to locate for you? The one I've been trying to find for two weeks?" Anna lifted one eyebrow and planted a fist on her hip. "Well, I found her. She's been hiding at your house."

"Funny."

"I thought so."

Jackson leaned back in his desk chair. "Sorry. Never occurred to me that you'd still be looking for her."

"Your wish, my command," she said with a shrug. "That's how the employer/employee thing works."

"Not usually," he muttered.

"I heard that."

"Not surprising," he said with a grin.

She walked into the office, a woman completely sure of her position and not the least bit intimidated by the boss she sometimes treated like one of her own children. "So," she said, putting both hands on the edge of his desk and leaning in. "This nice woman calls, introduces herself as Casey Davis and asks me to let you know that she won't be home for dinner."

"Why not?" He straightened up, frowning.

"The funny thing is, I hear a baby crying in the background while Casey and I are chatting." Anna's eyes narrowed on him. "Care to elaborate?"

"Where's she going to be?" Jackson ignored her dig for information, as he was on a quest for his own.

Anna straightened up. "She said she had an appointment with a potential client."

"Client?" But she ran a silly little one-woman operation out of her house—his house. Why would she need to meet anyone about that? Couldn't she just do the meeting on the phone? And who was she meeting?

"That's what she said," Anna told him. "Then, she said that she would be dropping Mia off here with you about four."

He stood and immediately started looking around his office, trying to spot potential danger zones. His gaze went from uncovered electrical outlets, to long cords, to the trash can, to…impossible. This was not a baby-proofed place.

"Who's Mia?" Anna's voice broke into his thoughts.

"My daughter," he said and heard the awe in his voice as he said the words. He'd had that baby girl in his house for one week and already his priorities had shifted. Seeing

Mia's smile first thing in the morning was a bigger jolt to his system than his usual cup of coffee. Holding her before she fell asleep turned his heart into mush and seeing her tears was enough to bring him to his knees.

He was a man desperately in love with his child.

And completely at a loss over her mother.

"Your daughter?" Anna grinned hugely, sprang around the desk and wrapped Jackson up in a hard hug. "Why didn't you tell me? Why haven't I met her?"

"Yes, I just found out myself, and you will this afternoon at four," he said, answering all of her questions.

"This is great, Jackson," Anna said. Then her eyes clouded and her smile slowly faded. "Can't wait to meet the mysterious Cassiopeia and the no doubt beautiful Mia. But, what are you going to do about Marian?"

Scowling, he said, "Get her on the phone for me, will you? Guess it's time I made a date for Marian and I to have a chat."

As Casey steered the big black boat of an SUV down the road, headed for King Airfield, she had to admit it had been an amazing week.

She and Mia had, in a few short days, settled comfortably into Jackson's gorgeous mansion on the hill. It would have been difficult not to. Before she and Mia moved in, Jackson had hired a cook, a full-time housekeeper and then later offered to add a nanny to the staff. But Casey drew the line there. She didn't want strangers raising her child and Jackson had seemed pleased with her reaction.

The house itself was gigantic and though it took Casey

a couple of days to learn her way around, she had to admit that there was a warmth to the place she hadn't expected. The rooms were big, but decorated in a comfortable style. Overstuffed furniture begged to be curled up in. Window seats beckoned and shelves filled with books called to her.

And as far as her bedroom went, she'd never even dreamed of having such a lush, romantic room—not that she spent much time in it. Despite her better judgment, she hadn't been able to stay away from Jackson.

The man was completely her opposite in every way and yet, there was such a near-overwhelming magnetic attraction to him, she'd given up trying to fight it. Every night, after tucking Mia in, Casey and Jackson moved to his bedroom and there, they spent hours locked in each other's arms. In bed, their differences didn't seem to matter so much.

Which was just a little disturbing.

Casey felt herself falling for the man and even though she knew it was a gargantuan mistake, she couldn't seem to stop herself. Yes, he was bossy and arrogant. But he was also tender and sweet. He could make her insane by pushing all of her buttons and then at night, he pushed different buttons and made her crazy in a much nicer way.

But there was no future in this. She was clearly setting herself up for a huge fall come the end of six months. Jackson had no intention of falling for her and Casey knew it. Right now, she was convenient, that was all. "It's my own darn fault, too. I never should have let this start up. Idiot."

Her hands fisted on the steering wheel as she looked out over what seemed like a mile of gleaming black hood. Glancing in the rearview mirror at the mirror fastened in front of the baby seat, Casey could see her daughter's smiling face.

"You like your daddy, don't you?" she asked and Mia waved her bedraggled teddy bear in response.

Casey wasn't blind. She could see the rapport building between Jackson and his daughter. In fact, he was a much more involved father than she'd thought he would be. Which made her worry a little. The closer he got to Mia, the harder it would be for him to let her go at the end of six months. And what if he decided he didn't want to let Mia go? What then?

What if he fought for custody anyway?

"Oh, this is turning into such a big mess," Casey whispered and flipped her turn signal on at the entrance to the airfield.

The field was, as were all things King, *big*. She drove straight up to the tower where Jackson's office was located and parked. When she got out of the car, the first thing she noticed was the noise. Jet engines rumbling, men shouting, and a loudspeaker calling for maintenance.

Getting Mia up and out of her car seat, Casey walked quickly to the building and slipped inside. Worrying about tiny eardrums around so much noise put speed into her steps. The tower building itself was carpeted and sleek, with chrome-and-black furniture and an elevator tucked into the back wall. A security guard took her name, ushered her into the elevator car and just before the doors closed, gave Mia a wink.

When the doors swished open again, an older woman was standing there beaming at them. Her short brown hair was stylishly cut, her beige slacks and white shirt looked crisp and professional and her brown eyes veritably twinkled.

"You must be Cassiopeia," she said, already reaching for the baby. Mia leaned out happily, eager to explore a new face.

"Casey, please."

"Of course," the woman said. "I'm Anna. Jackson's assistant and you, you little beauty, must be Mia King."

"Mia Davis," Casey said quickly, just to keep things straight.

Anna shot her a look, then smiled. "My mistake. Well, the boss is right on through there," she waved a hand at a closed door. "Why don't you go on in and I'll take care of Mia."

Her daughter looked completely at home on Anna's hip and the older woman clearly was enjoying herself, but still, Casey hesitated. "Are you sure?"

"Oh, yes. Don't worry. I've had four of my own and I didn't break one of them." Anna paused thoughtfully. "I did consider breaking the youngest, but changed my mind at the last minute."

Casey smiled, mother to mother and felt better immediately. "Okay then, I'll just tell Jackson I'm leaving and—"

"Take your time…." Anna had already turned away and was busily pointing out all of the airplanes to a cooing Mia.

Casey knocked lightly, opened the office door and stepped inside. Jackson was on the phone and she almost backed out, but he held up a finger and motioned for her to come in.

"That's right. We'll need the fuel delivered by tomorrow morning at the latest. We've got several flights booked for the weekend. Right." He nodded, made a note on the ledger in front of him and nodded again. "Good. See you then."

He hung up, then stood up, coming around the edge of the desk toward her. Shooting a glance at the closed door, he asked, "Mia with Anna?"

"Yes. She swooped in and snatched the baby the moment we showed up."

"Well, don't worry. She's in good hands."

Casey nodded and walked around the office. She'd wondered what this place would look like. And now, she saw it suited Jackson completely. A bank of windows to open up the world for him, wide desk, comfortable furniture and on the walls, paintings of King Jets. She turned to look at him. "You don't mind watching Mia while I keep my appointment?"

"No, but who's the appointment with?"

She blinked at him. "I'm sure you don't know him."

"Him?"

Did his tone just change? She shook her head. "Yes, him. Mac Spencer. We're meeting at Drake's for coffee. He wants me to design a new brochure for his travel agency."

"I know him," Jackson said, folding his arms across his chest and leaning back to sit on the edge of his desk. "His agency's in Birkfield."

"That's right."

"So how'd he find out about you? You live in Darby."

"Not anymore," Casey reminded him, still strolling the room, inspecting the stack of flight magazines on the narrow coffee table. "Mia and I took a walk through Birkfield a couple of days ago. I passed out business cards to the shop owners. Seemed like a good idea," she said. "And clearly, it was. It's already paid off."

And it made her feel good. She might be living in Jackson's little palace, but she made her own way in the world. Always had. Once this time with him was over, she'd be back on her own, providing for Mia. The more clients she had, the better their lives would be.

"That explains it," Jackson muttered, springing up off the edge of his desk as if he had a fire under his behind.

"Explains what?"

"Mac Spencer probably took one look at you and decided to have you for dessert," Jackson said tightly.

"Excuse me?" She stared at him and was astonished to see that his jaw was clenched and his brows were drawn low over dark eyes that were flashing with heat.

"He's notorious in town." Jackson stalked across the room, took hold of her arm and Casey did her best to resist the pull of the heat she'd come to expect from his touch. "He's got so many notches on his bedpost it's a wonder it's still standing."

"Notches?"

"God, Casey," he muttered, looking down into her eyes. "You can't be seriously considering going to meet this guy one on one."

"Of course I am," she said, tugging her arm free of his tight grasp. "This is *business,* Jackson. *My* business. I was doing this before you came charging into my life and I'll be doing it long after you're gone. I'm the sole support of me and my daughter."

"Not anymore you're not."

"Do you seriously think I'm just going to stand back and do nothing for the six months Mia and I are with you?"

"Why not? Call it an extended vacation."

"If I did that," she explained patiently, "I'd lose my clients and I can't afford that. People depend on me to come through for them. I take my job every bit as seriously as you take yours."

He looked like he was chewing on that one for a second. "Fine. *I'll* hire you."

"To do what?"

"Brochures," he said. "Magazine ads. You say you're good, prove it. Work for me."

A little zip of excitement skittered through her, as she considered the possibilities of working on an account like King Jets. She'd be way out of her depth, she knew, but she was good at layout, design, color and flash. She could do a great job for him and—she looked up into his eyes, and read the victory shining in those dark depths. Instantly, Casey quashed her little vicarious thrills. He didn't mean this. Any of it. He didn't know anything about her talents or her work. He was simply doing his best to make decisions for her. Again.

"If you're serious," she said, sliding the strap of her purse up onto her shoulder, "then we can talk about it. *After* I meet with Mac Spencer."

"You're. Not. Going."

She laughed shortly. "Yes. I. Am. And you can't stop me. You don't have the right. So," she added as she marched quickly across his office to the closed door, "you and Mia have a good time and I'll see you back at the house later."

Fifteen minutes into her "meeting" and Casey knew Jackson had been right about Mac Spencer. The man was sleaze. Oh, he was good-looking enough in a sharp, on-edge kind of way. His hair was perfectly styled, swept back from a high forehead. His eyes were blue and his jaws carried just the right amount of stubble to make him look rugged.

But their coffee hadn't even been served before he'd reached across the table to take her hand in his. Casey had pulled away and opened her portfolio, determined to make the kind of business contacts she would need. If she could convince this man that she could do the job, then she was willing to put up with his not-so-subtle flirtations. After all, it wasn't the first time she'd had to peel an overeager would-be client off of her.

But he was getting irritated at the way she kept sloughing him off. He waved one manicured hand at her still open portfolio, dismissing it. "This is all fine, but I think you'd get a better idea of what I'm looking for if we went back to my office. I could show you last year's plan and you could convince me how to improve on it."

No way was Casey going to go to his office with him. She already knew it was a one-man operation, which meant that she would be alone with him. Not something she had any interest in. Much better to stay in the safety of Drake's diner.

"If you'll look at this brochure I did for the Rotary Club of Darby last year, you can see that through the judicious use of color…"

He plucked the brochure from her hand and tossed it aside. Leaning across the table, he ran the tips of his fingers down the back of her hand in a slow stroke no doubt meant to be incredibly sexy. What it was, was irritating.

"Why don't you let me buy you dinner then? Some

place nice. Some place quieter. Where we could get to know each other a little better?"

"I really don't—"

"Evening, Mac."

Jackson's deep voice thundered out around them and had Casey jolting in her seat. She lifted her head to see him standing beside their table, his black, furious gaze shifting from Mac's hand on hers to the man himself.

"King," Mac said, straightening up a little, giving Jackson an uneasy smile. "What're you doing here?"

"Came to pick up Casey," he said tightly, leaning on the table and pinning Mac with a black stare that had the man clearing his throat and looking for an escape route. "You about done?"

"Sure. Yes. I'm sure I've got all I need," Mac said, looking from Jackson to Casey and back again like a man looking for an escape and not finding one. Finally, he slid from the booth and quickly scuttled backward, out of Jackson's arm reach.

"You've got all you're going to get, that's for sure," Jackson told him.

Nodding, Mac stiffened his shoulders, lifted his chin and sent Casey one withering look. "Thanks for the information, Ms. Davis. I'll be in touch."

As Mac left, Casey heard Jackson mutter, "Like hell you will." Then he sat down in Mac's empty seat across from her and smiled thinly.

"What was that about?"

"I was saving your ass."

"Did it look like I needed saving?"

"Actually, yeah."

Maybe it had, she thought now, wondering if the distaste she'd been feeling for Mac Spencer had shown on her features. But whether or not that was the case, she could have handled the situation on her own. "Well, I didn't."

"You don't have to thank me, but you could at least admit you needed me."

"Thank you?" She shook her head as she gathered up her portfolio, shuffled all of her extra papers and designs inside and then snapped it shut. "You probably just cost me what could have been a great job. This is my work, Jackson. Do I come onto the airfield and tell you which plane to fly? Or which pilot to hire?"

"No, but that's hardly the same thing."

"Of course it is." She slid out of the booth, grabbed up her portfolio and purse and looked down at him through narrowed eyes. "I could have handled that guy, Jackson. Do you think he's the first one to think he could lay hands on me? Do you think that's the first time I've had to take care of myself in a dicey situation? Well, it's not. I've done pretty well for myself my whole life and I can continue to do it. Without your help."

The fact that she was right had little to do with anything. She had been on her own for most of her life. He'd learned that early on. She had no family. No close friends but Dani Sullivan.

But now she had him.

For however long this lasted, she damn well had *him*.

When she stalked down the crowded busy aisle, Jackson bolted from the booth to follow. He dodged around a waitress balancing a tray of soft drinks and kept his eye on Casey as he walked.

His gaze locked on the sway of her hips in that short yellow skirt and then followed the line of her trim, tanned legs down to the three-inch heels she wore to give her more height.

He'd been furious when he walked up to the table to see Mac touching her. There'd been nothing he wanted more than to plow his fist into the man's face. And damned if he'd apologize for it.

He was right behind her when she left Drake's. An ocean wind raced at him as if it was trying to push him back inside. He squinted into the wind and the dying sunlight, held the door open for an elderly woman, then trotted after Casey before she could get into the SUV and take off. "Where's Mia?" she demanded.

"With Anna," he snapped. "She's perfectly safe."

"You were supposed to be the one watching her."

"I was too busy watching *you*."

"Which isn't your job," she reminded him.

"Like hell it's not," he growled, low in his throat as he grabbed her upper arms and yanked her in close.

The sun was setting and the weird half-light made her eyes gleam and her blond hair shine like spun gold. Her breath was coming fast and furious and his own heart was pounding erratically in his chest. "You think I couldn't see what Mac was thinking, planning? You think I'm just going to stand by and watch as some guy puts his hands on you? Ain't gonna happen, Casey. *Nobody* touches you but me."

Eight

The kiss was sudden and nearly violent in the desperate passion spilling from him. Casey's brain short-circuited around a dozen dizzying thoughts. She should stop him. She should pull away and tell him he had no say in who touched her. That she didn't need him watching over her. She should remind him that their only connection was Mia. She should say that just because they slept together didn't mean he owned her.

She did none of that.

Instead, she wrapped her arms around his neck, groaned into his mouth and surrendered to the fire. His grip on her gentled but the need didn't.

The heat was all-encompassing, devouring her, body and soul. His touch as he closed his arms around her middle and held her pressed tightly to him sent waves of awakening desire pulsing through her system. It was this way every time he touched her now. Since that first night together in his house, since he'd somehow shaken her loose from the life she'd thought she knew so well. One touch and she was his. One kiss and she wanted more.

Even knowing that it would all end.

She couldn't stop the need for him. Didn't want to.

Finally, he pulled his head back and they both gasped for air. She looked up into his dark eyes and saw the same raw passion she felt reflecting back at her.

"He touched you," he said, lifting one hand to stroke her cheek. There was fire in his eyes, more than sexual heat, a kind of possessiveness that touched Casey on a deep primal level.

"He put his hand on you and in his mind, he was doing much more."

"You can't hang a man for his thoughts, Jackson," she teased, sensing rightly that the storm was passing.

"Doesn't mean I can't want to." He cupped her face between his palms and the heat of his touch sifted down into her bones. "You make me crazy, you know that, right?"

It staggered her to admit to herself just how much she'd wanted to hear him say he loved her. And that not hearing it was a kind of pain she'd never known before. Then the truth hit. How ridiculous to realize, while standing in a diner parking lot, that she was in love for the first time in her life. She loved alone, that she was sure of and the ache in her heart pulsated heavily.

Trying for reason, trying for balance, she whispered, "Jackson, what're we doing?"

"Damned if I know." Shaking his head, he looked into her eyes and she read confusion there. Well, that was something, wasn't it?

Then he took a step back, slapped one hand to the SUV and said, "I don't like the idea of you working."

"Yeah, I got that," she said, almost amused by the stubborn glint in his eye and the disgusted curve to his mouth. Maybe it was better that they don't talk about what lay unspoken between them. It was certainly safer for Casey. She couldn't tell him she loved him without risking seeing rejection in his eyes. Without the pain of watching him try to distance himself.

So in the interests of self-preservation, she kept it light. "But I do work. And I won't stop that just because I'm living in your house now."

"Right." He ground his teeth together, looked out into the distance for a long moment, then shifted his gaze back to hers. "But if you were busy enough with a big client, you wouldn't have to go out drumming up business, right?"

Wary now, she tipped her head to one side and studied him. "What are you getting at?"

"Just answer the question."

"Okay, sure." She nodded as she thought about it. "If I had a big client, of course I'd devote my time to him—or her. But the fact is I don't, so I have to spread myself around."

"Not anymore."

"Jackson..." She had a feeling she knew where this was going. And though a part of her was thinking *yippee*, another, more sensible part was warning her not to go down this route with him. If she got in any deeper with Jackson, then the eventual break would be just that much harder, wouldn't it? But even as she thought it, she knew that she couldn't get any deeper than love.

Then he started talking and Casey could feel herself getting caught up in his plans.

"I meant what I said earlier," he told her, words rushing from him as if he were half convinced if he took too long, she'd end the conversation. "I *do* need new brochures and business cards and maybe a Web site—can you do Web sites?"

"Yes, but—"

He stepped in close, ran his hands up and down her arms and gave her a half smile she was sure he meant to be charming. God help her, it was.

"Think about it, Casey. Work for King Jets and be able to cut back everywhere else. Spend more time with Mia…"

"That's cheating," she pointed out.

His grin widened. "And, I'd like to point out that King Vineyards also has a Web site that needs a redesign—trust me, Travis can't do it himself and Julie's too busy opening her bakery to worry about stuff like that. Then there's the vineyard brochures, tasting menus, event notices…" He stopped, then added, "Julie, too! The new bakery. She could probably use your help in getting notices out about the bakery."

Her brain started racing. She couldn't help herself. Being able to list working for the King family on her résumé meant she'd be able to grow her business substantially. And she'd make more money and wouldn't have to take meetings with people like Mac Spencer anymore. Jackson had been so right about that guy, not that she was going to admit *that*.

Plus Jackson was right about something else. If she did this, she would have more time for Mia. Not to mention the fact that when their six months at his home were over, she'd have a better chance at supporting herself and her daughter.

Because, like it or not, the truth was, whatever was between her and Jackson wasn't forever. It didn't matter that she was almost getting used to his dictatorial ways. Didn't matter that the chemistry between them was off-the-charts hot. Didn't even matter that she loved him.

The only thing that *did* matter was keeping in mind that Jackson had arranged this as a temporary measure. To let him get to know his daughter.

Jackson was still talking, warming to his theme. "And then there's Gina and her Gypsy horses. She's got a Web site too and is always complaining about how hard it is to keep it updated when she's dealing with Adam and Emma and the horses…."

It all sounded wonderful, Casey thought, but how much harder would all of this make the eventual ending between she and Jackson?

"I don't really like the look in your eyes right now," he said softly, his thumbs tracing smooth lines over her cheekbones. "For a second or two, you looked excited at the idea, then all of a sudden the light in your eyes went out."

She dredged up a smile, hoped it was plenty bright and forced lightness into her tone. She wouldn't give him a reason to regret their time together. She wouldn't give him the opening to allow pity in his eyes because she'd tumbled into love where she shouldn't have.

"I'm fine, Jackson," she said, shaking her head at him. "And though I really hate to admit this to you because you're already pretty insufferable about being right all the time…"

"Yeah? Well, it's good to be right." That smile again. The one that sent shivers down her spine.

She blew out a breath. Really, how could she have helped falling in love with him? "You really are impossible, you know?"

"So they tell me."

Casey sighed and for her own sanity, stepped out of his touch and held out her hand formally.

"What's this?"

"A business deal," she said, smiling at his confusion. "You offered me a job, right?"

"Yeah, I did."

"Well then, I accept. I'll work for King Jets and for King Vineyards, and King Gypsies if Travis and Gina are interested—"

"They will be," Jackson promised as he took her hand in his and folded his long, warm fingers around hers. Then slowly, inexorably, he pulled her toward him. "But as far as sealing the deal goes," he murmured as he lowered his head to hers, "I prefer the term *sealed with a kiss*."

"Dani, when he kissed me, I swear my hair curled and you know it's too short to curl."

"Tell me," her friend demanded, her voice husky over the phone.

"We were standing there in the parking lot and he was all furious about that client making a move on me—"

"Sleaze bucket," Dani put in.

"Absolutely," Casey agreed. "Anyway, he—Jackson he, not the sleazeball he—grabbed me, pulled me up against him and kissed me so hard and so long and so deep, I'm pretty sure I felt his tongue on my tonsils."

"Wow, did it just get hot in here?"

"It's pretty damn hot here," Casey told her.

"Did he hold on really tight and just mush you in really close?" Dani asked on a sigh.

"Oh yeah."

"God, I love when Mike does that to me, but usually I have to get him really mad for that to happen."

"Jackson was mad all right."

"Worth it though, wasn't it?"

"Big time," Casey said and folded her legs up under her on the cushioned window seat in her bedroom. "But right about then is when I realized I'm in serious trouble."

"You did it, didn't you?" Dani sighed again. "You went and fell in love with him."

Casey turned her head to stare out at the spring storm. Lightning flashed behind black clouds and rain slashed at the window glass. The world outside was a blurred confusion of color that suited Casey's mood right down to the ground. And with Mia down for a nap and Jackson off at some meeting, she could indulge in the swamping emotions churning through her.

"Yeah," she said, grateful she had someone she could admit it to. "I so did. I love him."

"Oh, God." Dani's voice dropped in sympathy and Casey was reminded again of just how good it was to have a friend who understood *everything*. "Did you tell him?"

"What am I, crazy?"

A choked-off laugh shot from Dani's throat. "How does he feel?"

"I don't know." Casey sighed, watching the rain run in tiny rivers down the glass until it looked like the house was crying. "And I can't exactly ask, you know?"

"Absolutely not," Dani agreed, then half covered the receiver with her hand and ordered, "Mikey, I said we'd give the dog a bath later. Please stop squirting him with dishwashing soap."

Casey chuckled and it felt good. She'd needed this talk with Dani. In the time she'd been at Jackson's house, she'd been so caught up in him and Mia and finding time for her own work, that she hadn't called her friend as she should have. Dani might have kept her sane. Dani might have given her enough good advice to keep Casey from falling in love with the completely wrong man.

But even as she thought that, she knew that nothing could have changed the current situation. It was what it was. What had Jackson said when he first took her to bed? *From that first night, we were destined for this?* Well, maybe Casey had been destined to love him, too. That's how it felt. As if she'd finally found what she'd been searching for all her life.

For all the good it did her.

"What're you going to do?"

"What can I do?" she countered, smoothing one finger

down the windowpane, following the trail of a single raindrop. "I agreed to six months. If I tried to leave early, he'd try to take Mia."

Shock colored Dani's voice. "You think he'd still do that?"

Probably not, she mused. But how could she be sure? "I guess I'm not really sure about it, but can I afford to risk it?"

"So what's the plan then?"

"Good question. And there only seems to be one answer that I can come up with."

"Which is?"

"Enjoy what I have while I have it," she said firmly. "I may not have him forever, but I can relish this feeling, this time with him as long as I can, right?"

"Absolutely," Dani said, earning the title of Best Friend one more time. "So. Do I get any sordid details?"

Casey laughed and felt a little of the ache in her heart lift. "Sure, how many do you want?"

"How many do you have?"

"*Hundreds*," Casey admitted, her skin heating up, just remembering all the times she and Jackson had come together.

"Oh, honey. *Spill.*"

"You have a *what?*"

"A daughter," Jackson said, watching Marian's brown eyes narrow. He'd known this wasn't going to be easy, but he'd had Anna set up this meeting with Marian because it had to be done. He'd already put off facing her with the truth for too long. "I have a *daughter.*"

As he explained what had recently happened in his life,

telling Marian about how Casey and Mia had come to be living with him, she stood there looking at him as shocked as if he'd ridden a camel into the family home. Her brown hair swept to her shoulders in a smooth, turned-under style, and when she shook her head in disbelief, he saw that hair swing out, then settle back perfectly into place again.

He blew out a breath and turning, walked a few steps to the window overlooking a formal garden. Lines of hedges neatly trimmed, trees twisted into caricatures of what they should be and flowers so rigid they marched in line like an army battalion. Hell, even the rain seemed to be falling more neatly here than anywhere else.

Nothing relaxed or easygoing about the Cornice household. The interior was just as rigid and unforgiving as the gardens. Here, stately antiques reigned. Uncomfortable chairs, spindly tables and glass knickknacks that looked so fragile, it made a man uneasy just being in the room.

Jackson turned his head to look back at the woman he was supposed to marry and tried to remember why it had seemed like such a good idea at the time. But he couldn't. Because looking at Marian with her designer clothes and her stick-figure body made him think about curvy, luscious Casey in her worn jeans and oversized T-shirts.

He must be losing his mind.

"Her name is Mia," he said. Marian hadn't been taking the news well, but then he hadn't really expected her to. Why should she? "She's ten months old, I have a picture if—"

Marian held up one perfectly manicured hand. "No. Thank you. I'm not interested in your illegitimate child."

He bristled, fought down his temper and told himself

she had every right to be pissed off. But if she took another dig at Mia, all bets were off.

He'd put off telling Marian about Mia for too long, he knew that. He should have been up front with her about the change in his life right from the beginning. But the truth was, he hadn't been looking forward to this conversation for a couple of reasons. One being that he'd known how Marian would react—not that he could blame her, and secondly, he hadn't wanted to admit even to himself that there was a part of his life that didn't include Mia and Casey.

That was a dangerous path for a man like him. He'd never thought to get tied up in knots over anyone or anything. But there was no going back now.

"And you say the child and its mother—"

"*Her* mother—" Damned if Mia would be dismissed as an "it."

"—are ensconced in your house?"

"They're living there with me, yes." He walked back to her and as he got closer, noticed the pinched tightness around her mouth. Was she just mad, or was she hurt? He'd rather not think about having hurt Marian. Hell, he'd never hurt any woman he'd been involved with. There was never a reason to go out of your way to bruise hearts. You went into a relationship, you had as much fun as you could together, then as two adults, you said goodbye. No hard feelings. No regrets.

Something slithered through his mind at that thought though and he wondered how parting from Casey was going to go. She was so deep into his blood, into his mind, she was the only woman he'd ever been with who refused to leave his thoughts. She haunted him day and night. At odd moments, her image would pop into his brain to tease him, taunt him, remind him just how badly he wanted her.

Like now, for instance.

He shut down that train of thought and told himself it wasn't wise to deal with one woman while thinking about another one.

"I need some time with Mia—my daughter," he said. "I've missed too much already and I don't want to miss any more. I have to have some time, to figure out how we fit into each other's lives."

"I see," Marian said and walked slowly toward a sideboard where she poured herself a splash of brandy and then tossed it down her throat like medicine. "And the mother?"

"Well of course she moved in too, I couldn't very well separate them, could I?" Frustrated now, because it seemed she was deliberately making this harder than it had to be, Jackson said, "It's only for six months."

"And you want us to wait to get married until they're gone."

Gone. Well, hell. He didn't really want to think about that yet. How the hell could he live in that house, walk past Mia's room and know she wasn't in there? How would he be able to walk down that hall and not see Casey pinned up against the wall whimpering in ecstasy?

Damn, this was a mess. But, one problem at a time.

"Marian, I know we had an agreement—"

"Yes, we do," she said, turning around to face him again, one long pale hand resting on the curved neck of the Baccarat crystal decanter. "One I have every intention of honoring. The question is, will you?"

That was the question, he supposed. He'd come here this afternoon fully intending to go through with the marriage merger—all he'd wanted to do was wait six months. Now, he wasn't so sure. In fact, the longer he thought about it, the less inclined he was to honor the deal they'd made what now seemed like another lifetime ago. But he'd already thrown Marian a hardball this morning. Wasn't one enough at the moment?

"We'll talk about it again in six months," he said smoothly, not exactly answering her.

She looked him dead in the eye and for a second there, Jackson was sure he was going to see her finally lose her temper. Finally see some real honest-to-God emotion coming from the woman. But true to form, she backed off, did a mental count to ten and smoothed herself out again.

"I'm not happy about this, Jackson."

He nodded. "I can understand that. But there's no way around the situation." He pushed both hands into his slacks pockets and offered, "In fact, I'll understand if you'd prefer to call the whole thing off."

Something sparked in her eyes, but it was gone before he could identify it. "Of course not," she said. "An agreement was reached and I'll certainly do my part to honor it. As you said, we'll discuss this again in six months."

It would have been so much easier all the way around if she had simply ended their arrangement then and there. But maybe she wanted a little space to do it in her own way. And if that's what she needed, Jackson would give it to her.

As for him, the relief that welled and rippled through his body at the thought of postponing a marriage to Marian

Cornice was enough to tell him that when they had their next discussion, if she hadn't ended their arrangement, he would.

Marriages of convenience didn't always work, he told himself, despite how well things had turned out for his brothers. And thanks to the appearance of Mia and Casey in his life, he'd just managed to escape a marriage that he could see now would have been a misery.

There would be no merger with Cornice airfields after all and he was suddenly okay with that. King Jets had been doing nicely up until now and would continue to do so.

"Fine then. Now, if you'll excuse me…" Jackson turned to leave. He'd only taken a few steps when Marian's voice stopped him.

"Are you sleeping with her?"

"Don't do this," he said, turning to look at her. "To either of us."

"It's just a question, Jackson."

"One I'm not going to answer." He wasn't going to discuss this with Marian. Frankly, since they weren't engaged, it was none of her business who was in his bed.

"You just did answer it," she pointed out.

"Marian," he said, thinking that maybe now was the time to end this after all. Why drag it on for another six months? Make it a clean break, he told himself. Walk away a free man.

But she cut him off before he could say anything more.

Her features went smooth as glass. "Never mind, Jackson. Forget I asked. Now, if you don't mind, I'd prefer to be alone."

He wanted to say something but what the hell was left?

Hadn't he done enough damage already? He let himself out the front door and quietly closed it behind him. Rain pelted him, but it felt damn good after being in that overheated and yet cold-as-hell house.

He paused on the front step, lifted his face to the sky to let the rain wash over his face and from inside the house, he could have sworn he heard the nearly musical tinkle of crystal shattering.

Nine

"**S**he's got good ideas," Travis acknowledged a few days later, lifting a glass of King Vineyard Merlot. He sniffed the bouquet, smiled to himself and indulged in a sip.

Adam took a drink of his brandy and rolled his eyes at Travis's wine connoisseur behavior. "Gina's already cooing over the changes Casey suggested for her Gypsy Web site." He shook his head. "Been following me around the ranch for two days, talking my ears off about nothing else."

"That's good," Jackson said, pausing for a gulp of his favorite Irish whiskey. He felt a quick stab of pride in the fact that Casey had so easily come up with new, fresh ideas for the King family businesses. Plus, there was an extra added bonus to her working for the family. "It'll keep her busy."

"That all this is?" Adam asked from his seat on the leather couch in his study.

Jackson stood up, walked to the fireplace and stared down into the flames as they licked and curved over the dry logs stacked in the hearth. "What else could it be?" He turned his back to the flames then and looked from one brother to the other before saying, "She had a meeting with Mac Spencer a couple of days ago."

"Is that guy still trolling in Birkfield?" Travis demanded.

"Hell yes," Adam said. "I actually caught him looking at Gina when she leaned into the car to get Emma out of her car seat." The memory of it must have been enough to make him angry all over again, since Jackson saw his oldest brother's jaw clench. "Never wanted to hit a man so badly in my life."

"Did you?" Jackson asked, wondering if his brother had had the satisfaction denied him.

Adam sighed, disgusted, and took another drink. "Gina wouldn't let me. Said I'd get my hands dirty by slugging anybody that nasty."

"Would've been worth it," Travis mused. "A damn public service."

"That's what I said," Adam muttered, then shifted a look at Jackson. "Did *you* hit him?"

"Came close," Jackson admitted wistfully and silently added that he still wished he had. Just the idea of that bastard looking at Casey, touching her hand… "He ran so fast, I'd have had to chase him down though and I was too busy arguing with Casey."

"One day, some husband's going to get to lay that guy out on the sidewalk," Travis said and smiled dreamily, clearly hoping he would be the lucky winner.

Jackson looked at his brother and realized how much Travis had changed over the last year or so. Once, he'd been interested only in his wines and a string of uncomplicated beauties who sailed in and out of his life in a steady stream. Now, he was settled. With Gina and their daughter Katie.

"Hope I'm there to see it," Adam muttered.

"Me too," Jackson said, letting go of musings about his brother to savor the idea of smashing a fist into Mac Spencer's face.

"Did we care this much about that guy *before* we had women in our lives?" Travis asked no one in particular, then answered his own question. "Women sure liven things up, don't they?"

"That's one way of putting it," Jackson said, staring now into the amber liquid in his crystal tumbler.

"Not that talking about our women or dreaming about punching Mac out isn't a good time," Adam said into the silence, "but Jackson, was there a particular reason you wanted this meeting? Everything okay over at King Jets?"

"What? Oh, yeah. Fine." Jackson grimaced a little and said, "Well, I'll need to hire another pilot soon. Dan Stone is going to quit. His wife's scared and he won't let that go on much longer."

"Good man," Adam said, with a shake of his head. "I like Dan and I know he loves flying as much as you do, but it's right he put his family first."

Jackson lifted a brow. Wasn't that long ago that Adam had been devoted solely to the King ranch. But he guessed Gina had changed everything for Adam. Brought him back from the despair he'd hidden away in. His wife and daughter had given Adam exactly what he'd been lacking. Made him care about something more than the land and his brothers.

"But," Adam was saying, "I don't see how you needing to hire more flyboys has anything to do with us."

"It doesn't." Jackson stalked over to the closest chair, and dropped into it. Damn it, he didn't want to think about how much his brothers had changed. How everything seemed to be changing, including himself. For one damn minute he wanted the world to stand still so he could make sense of it again. But since that wasn't going to happen... "I came to tell you I went to see Marian this afternoon. Told her I wouldn't be marrying her anytime soon."

Both of Travis's eyebrows lifted. "You broke it off?"

"No," Jackson told him. "I didn't want to dump it all on her at once," he admitted. "I told her I needed six months. Told her about Mia and Casey and I figure I'll let Marian be the one to call it off. I owe her that much, anyway. But either way, the marriage isn't going to happen."

"Thank God," Travis said, a half smile on his face as he took another drink of wine.

"What's that supposed to mean?" Jackson looked at him and waited.

"Nothing. Just," Travis shot a glance at Adam as if for support, then looking back at Jackson, he grumbled a little and said, "But man, I never could see why you wanted to entangle yourself up with her."

Stunned, Jackson looked at both of his brothers in turn.

Adam shrugged as if to say he agreed with Travis. "That what you think, too?"

"Hell, yes," Adam said and got up to pour himself another splash of brandy. At the wet bar, he turned his head, looked at his youngest brother and said, "Jackson, the woman's about as warm and loving as a rabid polar bear."

Jackson hunched deeper into his chair, stretched out his legs and crossed one booted foot over the other. "Notice neither one of you said anything when I first suggested marrying her for the merger."

"You're a grown-up," Travis said, leaping out of his chair to join Adam at the bar. He poured more of the ruby-colored wine into his glass, chugged a healthy dollop of it then said, "If you want to make an ass of yourself, who're we to speak up and stop you?"

"My brothers?" Jackson stood up too and glared at both men. "Hell, you two had marriages of convenience and they worked out fine. You're happy aren't you?"

Both of them shrugged and nodded.

"So why shouldn't I figure the same thing would work for me?"

"Might have if you'd picked someone more…" Travis stopped short of a description of Marian.

"Or someone less…" Adam's voice trailed off and he shut up too.

Shaking his head, Jackson looked at the two men who had been the one constant in his life. His family. The Kings stood together, everybody knew that. They supported each other. Protected each other.

They always had, anyway. And now the two of them were standing there admitting that they'd been willing to let him walk into a marriage they both thought was wrong?

"This is great," Jackson said, crossing the room in a few long strides. He stepped around the bar and grabbed up the Irish whiskey. One more splash was all he could afford if he was going to drive home in an hour. "Thanks for nothing."

"You wouldn't have listened to us anyway," Travis said.

"Always did have a head like a rock," Adam added.

"My own family doesn't say anything when they think I'm making a mistake."

Adam looked at Travis. They both turned to Jackson, but Adam spoke first.

"You want an opinion?" he asked. "Fine. Here's one. If you're looking for a marriage of convenience that has a shot in hell of working out, why not marry Casey?"

"Huh?" Jackson set his untouched drink down on the bar and stared at the oldest King brother. "The last time I looked Casey doesn't own any airfields."

"You're either the most stubborn of us or the dumbest," Travis said with a pitiful look in his eyes. "No, she doesn't have airfields, you moron. But she *does* have your daughter."

Jackson took a breath and held it. He'd only just slipped out of a marriage that would have been, he could see now, a disaster. And his brothers wanted him to slip his head into another noose? What the hell kind of family support was this, anyway?

"You're crazy. Both of you," he said, with a look at each of them in turn.

"We're crazy?" Adam countered. "You're the one who seems willing to settle for six months with your kid. You're the one who's willing to let Mia and Casey stroll out of your life when there's something you could do to stop it."

Jackson's chest tightened. He wasn't sure why. He only knew that it was suddenly hard to breathe. Yes, he cared about Casey. And he loved Mia. But marrying the mother of his child just to get his child didn't sound like the right thing to do either.

"You know," he said, "you guys sound like you've got all the answers. You're standing there giving me advice like you're experts on this stuff."

"We *are* married," Travis pointed out. "To women we love."

"Uh-huh," Jackson countered, forgetting about the damned whiskey and shoving both hands into his jeans pockets. "And let's just think a minute about how smoothly you guys handled things with your women."

"Just a damn minute," Adam told him.

"No you wait," Jackson said, turning on his oldest brother. "Think back, huh? Didn't you make Gina so damn miserable she ran all the way to Colorado? Wasn't going to come back, was she? Not until you groveled and begged your way back into her heart."

"I didn't grovel," Adam muttered, a muscle in his jaw ticking.

"You sure as hell did," Travis said, laughing now and shaking his head.

"Just like you," Jackson told him, his gaze fixing on the middle King brother.

"Excuse me?" Travis's eyes narrowed and his laughter fell away.

"You heard me. You didn't have the guts to admit you wanted Julie until she damn near died when that elevator fell."

Travis shoved him. "You don't know a thing about what happened between me and Julie."

Jackson didn't budge. His temper jumped inside, boiling and frothing as he looked at his older brothers. Sure their lives were good now, but it hadn't always been so and damned if he'd let them forget it.

"Yeah I do. And you know what, neither one of you is qualified for the job of advice god. So back off."

In the thundering silence that followed his short speech, all three of them glared at each other. Finally though, Adam spoke up. "He's got a point."

"Don't tell him that," Travis muttered, taking another sip of wine.

Jackson laughed, temper gone as fast as it had come and reached for his glass of Irish. He took a swallow, letting the heat slide down his throat and spread through his system. Looking at his now just a bit sheepish brothers, he shrugged, point made and enjoyed the renewed sense of camaraderie. "Damn, when did life get so complicated?"

"You know exactly when," Adam said smiling, lifting his own glass. "To the women."

"The women," Travis said wryly, clinking his glass to theirs.

"The women," Jackson agreed and shared a toast with his brothers. His friends.

* * *

"This is amazing," Dani said the following Saturday. She was holding baby Lydia, jiggling her on her hip and watching as her son Mikey carefully held Emma King's tiny hand and helped her walk across the crowded lawn. "Would you look at my gorgeous son? Why isn't he that nice to his baby sister?"

Casey laughed and did a little jiggling of her own as Mia started to fret. "Because Emma's new to him, he's a sweetie like his daddy and he's nuts about his little sister and you know it."

Dani flashed her a smile. "Okay, yeah. He is. Just hope he likes the new one as much."

Casey shrieked and reached out to hug her best friend. "You're pregnant again? That's so great!" Eyes cautious suddenly, she said, "It *is* great, right?"

Dani laughed. "Yeah, it's great. Mike's excited about it. Just look at him."

Casey's gaze swung to where Mike Sullivan stood among the King brothers, laughing and talking as they drank beer and grilled steaks on Jackson's shiny new barbecue. Her friend's husband did look every inch the contented male and Casey was glad he'd been able to take the day off to join them all for the picnic Jackson had suddenly decided to throw.

Her gaze fixed on the man most in her mind and she felt her heart give a little ache. He'd come to mean so much to her in the last month or so. She hadn't expected it. Hadn't wanted it. But the unthinkable had happened anyway. She'd fallen in love with a man she knew wasn't interested in forever.

"Uh-oh," Dani said from beside her. "I see that look. And if you don't want Jackson to see it, you'd better go to your happy place."

Chuckling, Casey tore her gaze from Jackson to focus on her friend again. "The problem with that suggestion is that Jackson *is* my happy place."

"Oh, honey, that just sucks."

More laughter. "Very eloquent."

"You know, there may be more to this relationship than you think," Dani said, squatting now to sit Lydia on the quilt spread out at their feet.

"I don't think so." Casey kneeled down, set Mia on the quilt beside Lydia and smiled at her daughter before saying, "Jackson was really clear right up front. He wanted six months. Well, one of those months is gone now. And he hasn't said anything about wanting to renegotiate. Hasn't mentioned that his feelings have changed…" Her gaze drifted, as it always did whether she wanted it to or not, to Jackson.

In the bright spring sunlight, his dark hair shone and his eyes glittered. Standing with his brothers and Mike, with smoke from the barbecue twisting and swirling about him in the wind, he almost looked as if he'd stepped out of a dream. He laughed and something inside her fisted. His gaze slipped to hers and she felt the immediate swell of response in her body.

She sighed and deliberately looked at Dani, watching her. "Oh," her friend said on a sigh, "you've got it really bad, don't you?"

"Afraid so," she said.

"Not hard to understand," Dani told her, waving one hand to indicate their surroundings. "This place is awesome. Jackson's gorgeous and he's crazy about your kid. You'd have to be made of stone to not be affected by it all."

Casey nodded and turned to smile up at the two women approaching them. "You're absolutely right about all of it, but let's change the subject, okay?"

"Oh. Right."

"Hi," Gina King said as she plopped down onto the quilt beneath the shade of an ancient elm tree. "Julie and I thought we'd join you two here, if that's okay."

"Of course it's okay," Casey said and smiled as Julie, nestling her infant daughter to her chest, sat down beside her.

"Your son is just the cutest thing," Gina said, grinning at Dani. "The way he acts with Emma just touches my heart."

Naturally, the surest way to win Dani's friendship forever was to praise one of her children. And as she settled in to talk babies with Gina, Casey watched as Julie opened her shirt to feed baby Katie.

"She's beautiful," Casey said softly, reaching out with one hand to trace a fingertip across the tiny girl's forehead. Already, Mia was growing up and Casey could see the day ahead when her little girl would no longer be her baby, needing only her. She would have liked to have more children, she thought longingly. But having Mia had been so expensive, the chance of repeating the experience was slim and she already knew that conceiving any other way was nearly impossible. But as she considered that, a new thought whispered through her mind and disappeared again when Julie started talking.

"Thanks, Travis and I think she's gorgeous, of course." Julie hissed in a breath when Katie latched onto her breast, then grinned and said, "I wanted to tell you again, how much I *love* your ideas for the bakery Web site."

Pleased, Casey smiled back, pushing regrets and worries out of her mind for another day. "I'm so glad. I think it's going to be fun getting the King family sites up and running."

"A woman after my own heart," Gina crowed. "Someone else who thinks work is fun! I swear, to hear Adam grumble you'd think I'm the only wife in the world who has a job. And I work right there on the ranch! He sees me every day."

"Mike does the same thing," Dani put in, "but some of that might be because we've become ships that only occasionally bump in the night!"

"Travis hates it too," Julie agreed with a small laugh. "He used that bakery of mine as a tempting offer to get me to marry him in the first place and now he grumbles because I want to spend so much time there." She laughed delightedly. "But then I remind him how hard it is to pry him out of the tasting room at the winery."

It felt good to be with these women, listen to them all complain lovingly about their husbands. But it also brought home a simple truth to Casey. She could complain all she wanted about Jackson, but she didn't really have the right, did she? He wasn't her husband. He was her lover.

Her *temporary* lover.

No matter how much she felt at home here, with these women, with the King family, at this amazing hilltop mansion, none of it really belonged to her.

"I'm thinking when this one's born," Dani was saying slyly, "that I just might come to Casey for a job." She slid a hopeful glance at her friend. "That way I can stay home with the kids and maybe Mike and I can see each other for more than a mumbled greeting in the hallway as we change shifts!"

"What a great idea," Gina put in. "I've got lots of plans for Casey's time, so I think she'll be needing the help."

"You've got plans?" Julie said with a laugh, shifting baby Katie from one breast to the other. "Back off, sister-in-law of mine, I've got the bakery getting ready to open and I want those menus done before the next tasting at the winery—"

Enjoying herself immensely, Casey gave them all a broad smile and clapped her hands. "As much as I love being the center of attention," she said, "there's plenty of me to go around." Then she shot a look at Dani. "As for you…we're going to have to talk, because if you're serious, I could use you *sooner* rather than later."

"Seriously?" Dani's eyes sparkled at the thought of being able to stay home with her kids.

"Definitely," Casey told her. With all the new work she had lined up, she was going to need the help. Who better than her best friend? "And as for the menus for the winery," she said, looking at Julie again, "I came up with an idea yesterday that I think you're going to love."

"Excellent!" Julie whooped with excitement and just for good measure stuck her tongue out at Gina. "I win. Can I see them now?"

"Sure." Casey stood. "Keep an eye on Mia and I'll run upstairs to get them."

With the women in charge, Casey sprinted across the

lawn toward the back door of the big house. She ran over the flagstone patio, pausing only long enough to wave at Jackson, then she slipped through the open French doors and into the shadowy coolness of the state-of-the-art kitchen.

The cook had the day off since Jackson was busily burning dinner on his own and so the house felt empty and quiet as Casey ran down the hall and up the stairs. From outside, the wash of voices and laughter floated to her on a soft wind and she smiled to herself as she ran down the hall to Jackson's bedroom. Temporary or not, she liked being a part of a big family. Since she'd been on her own for so many years, the idea of being surrounded by those you cared about was a delicious one.

She'd been showing Jackson the new design for the King Vineyard menus earlier that morning and she was sure she'd left the papers on Jackson's dresser. She entered the big room that smelled of him and saw what she was looking for right away. But out of the corner of her eye, Casey also noticed a new, economy-sized box of condoms lying in the middle of his neatly made bed.

"Oh, perfect," she muttered, shaking her head. If anyone in his family came upstairs for any reason, that would be the first thing they spotted. Just what she needed. Sure, they all had to know she and Jackson were lovers. That didn't mean she needed to draw them a picture, though.

Picking up the box, she opened his bedside table drawer to put them away. But the world stopped and the condoms fell from suddenly nerveless fingers when she found a small, dark-blue velvet jeweler's box tucked inside the drawer.

Mind racing, heart pounding, she held her breath, picked it up, opened the lid and stared down at a diamond that was so big it deserved its own zip code. It flashed in the light as if it had been waiting for someone to give it the opportunity to shine and Casey's mouth went dry at the implications.

Was Jackson going to propose?

Her heart leaped in her chest and an unexpected joy sent so many sharp, jagged shards of happiness through her it was nearly painful.

"Hey," Jackson said from the doorway, "what's going on? I saw you running and—"

She turned around, heart in her eyes and held up the box she'd found. And joy died as his smile faded.

"Oh, God," he whispered. "That's Marian's."

Ten

"Marian?" Casey's voice sounded so small, so hurt, Jackson felt her pain like his own.

He hadn't thought about that damned ring in weeks. If he had, he would have taken it to the bank, put it in the safety deposit box. But no, he'd been so wrapped up in Casey and Mia that he'd tossed the three-carat diamond into a drawer and forgotten all about it.

Until it had shown up to bite him in the ass.

"Damn it," he muttered, walking toward her. He took the velvet box from her hand, snapped it shut and dropped it back into the drawer. Then he slammed that drawer closed and looked into blue eyes that were so pale, so *wounded,* he felt like a first-class bastard.

"Um," she said, taking a sidestep away from him and looking everywhere but directly into his eyes, "I'm sorry. I didn't mean to pry. I was only putting the condoms away and—"

"Casey, let me explain." He reached for her, but she slipped away like mist before he could actually touch her. And just for a second, he wondered if it was a sign of things to come.

"Explain?" She choked out a laugh and backed up even further. Shaking her head, she walked quickly to his dresser and snatched up the pages she'd left there earlier. The designs she had for the King Vineyard menu. The ones she'd been so excited about that morning.

He remembered her showing them to him, with her eyes alight and her imagination on high gear. And even then, he'd felt a small twinge. He'd set her up with his brothers and their wives more for his convenience than for her sake. He'd wanted her safe. There. In the house.

Now, even her joy in the direction her business was taking had dimmed. Because of him.

"There's nothing to explain," she said and as she talked her voice got firmer, stronger. "You've got an engagement ring for another woman in the same drawer where you keep the condoms you use with me. What could be clearer? I'm the bedmate, she's the wife material." She headed for the door. "Trust me, I get the picture."

"No you don't," he snapped and cut her off before she could get out of the room, away from him.

From outside, he heard the rumble of his brother's voices, the laughter of the women clustered together beneath the tree and even the call of seabirds swooping low, looking for a handout.

But inside, all was cold and quiet. Looking into her eyes, Jackson felt the distance between them and damned if he could find a way to close it. He hadn't meant for her to find out about Marian. If everything had gone according to his plan, she and Mia would have stayed here for six months and then they all would have gone on with their lives.

But somewhere along the line, things had changed. He wasn't sure how, wasn't sure when and he for damn sure didn't know what to do about it. But Casey was staring at him and he had to say something.

"Yes, I had planned to marry Marian," he blurted when nothing better came to mind.

He saw her wince and if it had been possible, he'd have kicked himself. He'd never planned to hurt her. Yet it seemed he couldn't now avoid it.

"It was a business decision," he told her, trying somehow to lessen the sting of the surprise she'd just had.

She closed her eyes briefly, shook her head as if she were tired and said, "Business."

"Yes. A marriage of convenience. A merger really, more than a marriage," he added. Then he took a deep breath and kept talking because he sensed she was shutting down. Shutting him *out*. And suddenly, he very much wanted to be *in*. "Look, both of my brothers married women for the wrong reasons and wound up so damned happy they're annoying with it. I figured I stood at least the same chance they'd had and it was a good call for King Jets. Marian's father owns several well-placed airfields around the country. By marrying her, I guaranteed King Jets landing space and new routes."

"Good for you," she said, folding her arms over her

chest. "Congratulations. I'll be sure to get all the new routes correctly when I redesign your Web site."

He groaned with frustration himself. "The damn ring's here, remember? It's not on her finger because I'm not marrying her."

"Really. Why not?"

Why not. A loaded question if he'd ever heard one. And hell, he wasn't completely sure of the answer himself beyond the fact that he couldn't face the thought of a lifetime with a woman who wasn't Casey.

Damn.

When he didn't answer, Casey looked up at him, waiting. "It's a simple question, Jackson. Why are you not marrying the fabulous Cornice airfields?"

"Because of you and Mia," he said, tightening up in self-defense. The woman was glaring at him like he'd just told her he was personally responsible for the new sport of puppy kicking. "I told her I needed time. Time with Mia. Time to get my life together."

"So you're not marrying her *now*."

"Ever," he corrected, more certain of that fact now than he had been before.

"That's not what you told her though, is it?"

"No," he admitted, shoving one hand through his hair and wondering how the hell to get out of this mess he was slogging through. "I told her we'd talk in six months," he admitted. "I wanted to give her the chance to call it off herself."

"How very noble of you," she said and tried to step past him.

He cut her off again and she blew out a frustrated breath.

"It's not noble," he argued, trying to figure out how to explain to her what he didn't completely understand himself. "It's—"

"It's what, Jackson?" she asked and he actually *saw* her eyes go from pale to dark blue and he felt a wary twinge echo inside him. "Expedient? You don't want to be engaged to one woman while sleeping with another? Well, that just makes you a candidate for Man of the Year, doesn't it?"

Her hurt was quickly swallowed by fury and Jackson, being a wise man, took a step back.

"You used me," she said tightly, raking him up and down with a gaze that should have turned him to ice on the spot. "You used me for sex while keeping the no doubt eminently suitable *Marian* in the wings."

He was willing to let her blow off some steam, but damned if he'd stand there and let her insult both of them. "We used each other for sex, babe," he said and saw his verbal dart hit home. Quickly, instinctively, he followed it with another. "I never promised you anything."

"So that makes it okay, hmm?" Her whisper was nothing more than a hiss of sound. "Don't make promises and then it doesn't matter what you do? Who you hurt?" She walked in close, jabbed her index finger at his chest and said, "What about Mia? Were you going to push her aside once you married *Marian?*"

"Of course not! Mia's my daughter. She's always going to be my daughter."

"That's something, I suppose," she said under her breath.

"Casey…" He reached out and grabbed her shoulders,

holding onto her tightly when she tried to slip out of his grasp. He didn't know how to put things back together and it irritated hell out of him to have to admit that to himself. Always before, he'd known what to say. What to do. Now, when he needed that ability the most though, it had deserted him. "Don't do this. Don't do this to us. Don't ruin what we have."

"What we have?" she repeated softly. "You can't ruin what you don't have." When she lifted her gaze to his, he saw the furious dark blue of her eyes had faded to a nearly impersonal pale blue stare. "Besides, I didn't do any of this, Jackson. You did." She pulled away from him, tightened her grip on the papers she held in one fist and said, "Now. Julie's waiting to see these menus."

"She can wait a few more minutes," he said, not willing to let her go. Not when there was so much left unsaid between them. Not when he could still see pain he'd caused shining in her eyes.

"No, she really can't." Casey ran one hand over her short, shaggy hair, and said, "I'd rather your entire family and my friends didn't know anything was wrong, so if you don't mind, I'd like to see some of your fabulous acting skills when you go back downstairs."

"Casey—"

"No reason the day has to be spoiled for anyone else," she said and walked out of the room without a backward glance.

When everyone had left, Casey still was in no mood to talk to Jackson and since she needed to make a trip into town, she left him with Mia and took off. The drive in the big black bus he'd purchased for her at least shifted her concentration away from the fool she'd made of herself. She had to focus on the road, on other drivers, rather than on the lancing pain stabbing at her heart.

"It's your own fault," she murmured, steering the lumbering SUV into a diagonal parking slot in front of the drugstore. She slipped the gearshift into park, set the brake and turned off the key. Then she leaned her forehead on the steering wheel and closed her eyes. "You knew going in that this was temporary. That all it was for Jackson was a chance to know his daughter. You're the one who let sex become more. You're the one who started daydreaming…."

She blew out a breath, lifted her head and stared through the windshield at the store in front of her. A sinking sensation opened up in the pit of her stomach as she thought about why she was there. What she'd come to buy. And the fact that if she was right, everything was about to get much more complicated.

Jackson tried to talk to her when she got home, but she breezed right past him as if he weren't there. So he decided he'd give her a little space. A little time. Work things through in her head, then he'd talk to her again and she'd damn well listen.

He'd just spent the longest damned afternoon of his life, talking to his brothers and Mike Sullivan, pretending nothing was wrong, when he could *feel* Casey's misery hanging over him like a black cloud dripping rain. No one else had noticed, of course, because she'd plastered a smile on her face and had done just what she'd set out to do. Kept everyone else in the dark about what had happened between them.

"But what exactly did happen?" he muttered as he stared through the living room windows at the night beyond. "She found a ring I didn't use. Big deal. It didn't *mean* anything," he argued with himself, his voice a low mutter of disgust. "I told her I broke it off with Marian, why can't she understand that?"

Logic was lost on women, he thought. They were too busy being hurt or wounded or angry to listen to reason. Well, he told himself, she'd listen tonight, whether she wanted to or not.

He listened hard and heard Casey singing to Mia as she bathed the baby then put her to bed. Then he listened to the sounds of Casey moving around and realized for the first time that the reason he'd never spent much time in this house before now was that it had been too quiet. Too big for one man. Too filled with a silence that only seemed to get bigger when a man had time to think about it.

But with Mia and Casey here, the house seemed alive, somehow. And so, damn it, did *he*.

He finally gave up on trying to work out a new flight schedule, assigning pilots to fill in the gaps left by Dan, who had indeed quit right after the birth of his son. He'd worry about the logistics of flight time tomorrow. Jackson was definitely going to need to hire someone else, but until he did, he himself would have to pick up some of the slack.

Since Mia and Casey had come into his life, flying had taken a back seat. He hadn't been on a run himself in weeks and up until that very minute, he hadn't even realized it. Hadn't missed it.

Maybe his brothers were right, he thought suddenly. Maybe he should ask Casey to marry him. It would sure as hell solve a lot of problems. They shared Mia. And they shared an incredible chemistry that would make living together no hardship at all.

He smiled to himself as he warmed to the idea. Hell, Adam and Travis might have hit on the solution he needed. A marriage of convenience. But with the *right* woman.

"Jackson?"

His head whipped around and he jumped to his feet. As if his thoughts had conjured her, Casey stood in the open doorway of the living room. He hadn't heard her come downstairs because he'd been lost in his own thoughts. But now that he saw her, standing there in the wash of golden lamplight, she looked pale and her eyes seemed huge. Wide and shocked.

"What's wrong?" Before he even realized he'd taken a step, he was moving toward her.

"Nothing—" she waved him away, but he wouldn't be put off.

Dropping one arm around her shoulders, he steered her to a chair, pushed her down into it and tried to ignore the fact that she'd been so stiff and unyielding beneath his touch. Still mad, then. Well, fine. He could bring her around. In fact, as soon as he told her his idea, he had the feeling that she'd be so damn happy, all thoughts of this afternoon's confrontation would fall away.

He fell to a crouch in front of her and looked up into

her eyes. Eyes that were swimming in a sheen of tears she was fighting desperately to keep at bay. Worry rose up in him, nearly choking him and Jackson pushed his own plans to one side for the moment.

"Damn it, Casey, something's wrong," he said. "I can see it on your face. If this is still about what happened earlier, I want to talk to you about it. I've been doing some thinking and if you'll just hear me out—"

"Stop." Casey shook her head, scrubbed both hands over her face and then met his gaze with a grim determination that filled Jackson with a kind of dread he'd never known before.

"What is it?" he asked, reaching out and taking one of her hands in his. She was trembling. Damn it, what was going on? "Just say it, Casey."

"I'm pregnant."

Casey watched as shock, then wonder, then relief flashed across his eyes. She pulled her hand from his and sat quietly, waiting for him to say *something*.

Taking the home pregnancy test half an hour ago had solidified for her what she'd begun to suspect only that afternoon. Talking with the other women about babies and pregnancies, Casey had realized with a start that her period hadn't arrived on schedule. There had just been so much going on in her life lately, she hadn't paid the slightest bit of attention to the fact that her period simply hadn't shown up. And even if she had, she wouldn't have worried. After all, a doctor had told her that it would be nearly impossible for her to conceive the old-fashioned way. That's why she'd gone to a sperm bank in the first place. Why she'd had an in vitro procedure. How she'd come to be here, with a man who didn't love her.

The father of *both* of her children.

"I thought you said—"

She nodded, knowing what he was going to say. "My doctor told me it would be nearly impossible—" She laughed shortly and felt the sound scrape at her throat. "I guess the key word in that phrase is *nearly.*"

"So that first night when we—"

She nodded. "Apparently, your little swimmers have no trouble finding my womb."

He almost looked pleased, but maybe that was just her imagination working overtime.

"How long have you known?"

"Since about a half hour ago." She jumped up from the chair, suddenly unable to sit still a moment longer. Rubbing her hands up and down her arms, she paced aimlessly around the room. She could *feel* Jackson's gaze on her, and wished more than anything that she could throw herself into his arms and celebrate this…miracle.

She'd had no one but Dani to celebrate news of her first pregnancy. And this one was such a triumphant thing, such a one-in-a-million shot, that she wanted to shout, to laugh, to cry. But this time, she would do all of that alone, despite the fact that the baby's father was in the same room with her.

Casey couldn't fool herself any longer. She'd wanted to pretend that somehow, Jackson would one day come to love her. But the simple truth was, he didn't. Wouldn't. And it wasn't as if he were incapable of love. He loved Mia, that was obvious to anyone with eyes. So it was only Casey he couldn't love. And the addition of one more child wasn't going to change that.

"Casey."

She stopped, turned and looked at him from across the room.

"Don't you want the baby?"

"Of *course* I want this baby," she said, cupping both hands over her abdomen as if she could prevent the tiny life nestled inside from hearing any of this conversation. "This is a gift, Jackson. One I'll always treasure. It just…" she sighed and shook her head "…makes everything that much more complicated than before."

"No." He walked to her side, stopped directly in front of her and looked down at her. His eyes were shining, his smile was wide and when he spoke, Casey could hardly believe what he was saying. "This just makes things simpler," he said.

"I don't see how."

He ran his hands up and down her arms until finally sliding them up to cup her face between his palms. "That's what I wanted to talk to you about. I've got the solution to this, Casey. Marry me."

Eleven

"What?"

He'd surprised her, Jackson thought. Good. Better to keep her a little off balance. Better to force her to go with her instincts than to give her time to consider all options. Of course, when she finally *did* consider them, she'd see he was right. This was the absolute best decision for all of them.

"Marry me," he repeated, astonished at how easy the words fell from his mouth. Hell, he'd had an arrangement to marry Marian and he hadn't been able to talk himself into making the actual, formal proposal. But saying the words to Casey was different.

Right.

"You're crazy," she said, shaking her head and moving back, out of his touch, away from him.

So maybe keeping her off balance wasn't the best

option, he told himself, thinking fast. Maybe he should lay it all out for her. Clearly she was too muddled in her head right now, due to finding out about the coming baby.

Another baby.

Joy filled him. And pride. And a sense of expectation he never would have believed possible. He'd missed so much with Mia, Jackson couldn't wait to experience everything with this baby. He wanted to be there for all of them. He had to make Casey see that doing things his way made sense.

"It's perfect, don't you see?" He grinned and threw both hands high before letting them slap down against his thighs again. "We both love Mia. Now we've got a new baby coming. There's plenty of room in this house as you well know and you and I get along great."

She shook her head, staring at him as if he were speaking Greek. So he talked faster.

"You and I, Casey, we've got something good going. We can build a family here, with neither one of us being a weekend parent." He took a step closer and felt hope notch a little higher inside him when she didn't step back. "You've got all the new work for the King family and we'll add on to your office here at the house. Do it up however you want it. We can do this, Casey. We've got chemistry together, you have to admit that. We work well together, we both love our daughter, what could be better?"

She lifted one hand to her mouth, shook her head and looked at him as if he were out of his mind entirely. Why the hell wasn't this making sense to her? It was all perfectly logical. Reasonable.

"Love could be better, Jackson," she finally said on a tired sigh. "You were going to marry Marian—"

"Don't start on that again—"

"But you didn't think of marrying me until you found out I was pregnant. You don't want a wife, Jackson. Not really. You want company in bed and you want to be a father."

He frowned at her. This was not going the way he'd expected it to. "Even if you were right," he countered, "how does that make me any different than you? You said yourself you wanted to be a mother, that's why you didn't wait for a perfect relationship. You went to the sperm bank and got the child you wanted. Well, I *have* the child I want, right here. And now you tell me I'm going to have another one. So why wouldn't I want to be their father?"

"You're right," she said, but he didn't feel any better. "I wanted to be a mother. But the difference between us is, I didn't marry someone I didn't love to do it. Jackson, don't you see? The fact that you love Mia—that you will love this baby—isn't enough to base a marriage between us on."

"Why the hell not?" It sounded great to him. A ready-made family. Two people who liked each other, enjoyed each other.

"Look, you were all set for a marriage merger—"

"Will you leave her out of this? I told you, Marian doesn't mean a thing to me."

"Neither do I," she countered quickly. "This is just another convenient move for you. Before, you were going to use your marriage to expand your airline. With me, you'll expand your family. It's just another merger."

"With a hell of a lot better chance for survival," he told her.

"No, no it wouldn't work."

"Give me one good reason why not." He stared at her, completely lost as to her reaction. He'd been so sure she'd see that this was the right thing to do. So positive that he'd made the right move. That a marriage between them would solve all of their problems.

"Because I love you, Jackson." She gave him a sad smile. "I didn't mean to, and believe me when I say I wish I didn't, it would make things much easier."

He wasn't an idiot. He'd known that she had feelings for him. He hadn't really thought about her being in love with him, but since she was, why couldn't she see that it made even *more* sense for her to marry him?

"Now I'm really confused," he admitted with an under-the-breath curse. "If you love me, you should be *happy* with this solution."

"Happy to marry a man who loves my kid, but not me?" She shook her head. "Happy to live a lie? Happy to deny myself the hope of being loved in return? No, Jackson. Your idea doesn't sound like a bargain to me."

"Damn it, I *care* about you!" He took another step forward and she lifted her gaze to his. Her eyes were pale blue. No passion. No anger. No dark, churning emotion changing that color to a deep-sea blue. There was only regret shining in her eyes and Jackson felt as if he were standing on a slippery slope, skidding relentlessly downhill toward an abyss he couldn't avoid.

His chest tightened and everything in him went hard and

still. He felt as if he were fighting for his life. Why couldn't she just take what he had to offer her? A life with him and their kids? He cared more for Casey than he had ever allowed himself to care for anyone. Why couldn't it be enough?

He grabbed her shoulders, pulled her to him with a yank and folded his arms around her. She stood still for him, but she didn't wrap her arms round his waist. Didn't yield her body to his. Didn't lean into him. She was simply *there*.

"Caring isn't loving, Jackson," she whispered against his chest, her voice muffled so that he barely heard her words. "I deserve more."

"It's all I've got to give," he said.

"I know," she told him. "That's the saddest part about this."

He let her go then and his arms felt empty without her. *He* felt empty, damn it, and there was no reason for it. All she had to do was accept his proposal and they'd be fine. They'd have everything.

Why couldn't she see that?

When she walked past him, headed for the hallway, he called out and she stopped. "Where are you going?"

She turned her head to look back at him. "Upstairs. I'm tired and I need some time alone."

When she was gone and the only sound in the living room was the hiss and crackle of the fire in the hearth, Jackson thought that "alone" was overrated.

Early the next morning, Casey sat in the dining room, Mia tucked into her high chair, cheerfully mashing banana slices in her tiny fists. While watching her daughter have breakfast, Casey drank tea and wished for caffeine.

Laying alone in her bed had felt so strange. She was used to Jackson's touch, his heavy sigh as he settled into sleep. The drape of his arm over her middle as he pulled her up close. She'd come to rely on having him there beside her and now that he wasn't—she was lost.

Mia squealed, lifted both banana-covered hands and kicked at her high chair. Without even turning around, Casey knew that Jackson had come into the room. No one but he ever got that kind of reception from his daughter.

"Good morning." His deep voice rumbled through the room and seemed to reverberate around her. Instantly, Casey's heartbeat quickened and she felt a slow build of heat swirling inside her. God, would she always feel this way about him? Was she destined to spend the rest of her life in love with a man who only "cared" for her?

Steeling herself, she nodded. "Morning, Jackson."

"Sleep well?" he asked.

"No, you?"

"Great."

Disgusted, she shot him a look as he came around the table, bent down to kiss Mia and slid his gaze to hers. Instantly, she felt better. He was lying. There were shadows under his eyes that were every bit as dark as her own. Somehow, she enjoyed knowing his night had been long and miserable, too.

Sunlight slanted through the windows. Mia cooed and gurgled. And still Casey and Jackson stared at each other, each waiting for the other to speak first. Finally, Jackson did.

Pouring himself a cup of coffee from the carafe on the table, he said, "Last night you told me you needed some time to yourself."

All the alone time in the world wasn't going to solve the problems facing her. But she had to think. And being around Jackson was not conducive to thought. "I still do."

"Well, that's what I want to talk to you about." He paused for a sip of coffee. "You know I'm shorthanded at the airfield." She nodded. "Well, I've decided I'm going to take one of the flights myself. Give us both a little breathing room for a few days."

"A few days?" Strange, she'd wanted alone time, but hearing him say he was leaving wasn't making her happy. Apparently she wanted alone time with him nearby. God, she was a mess.

"Yeah," he said softly, "I'm heading to Paris this afternoon. I'm flying a couple over there, then I'll stay and take care of some business."

"Paris?" He was leaving. For days. The ache of loneliness settled in, but she told herself it was probably for the best. She wanted him to love her as much as he did their children. And the fact that he didn't made her feelings too raw and painful for her to be around him.

His voice dropped and Casey looked up into his dark eyes as he added, "As I recall, I once promised you a trip to Rome."

That night in the hall, she thought. The first night in this house with him, when they'd set the path they'd followed ever since. The night she'd discovered that her body could erupt in flames and she could survive to tell the tale.

"I remember." But fantasies and great—amazing—sex

didn't take the place of love. He wanted her, she could see it in his eyes. But want was a poor substitute for need. So it was good he was leaving, she told herself.

He set his coffee down onto the table, leaned both hands on it and speared her gaze with his. "Say the word and I'll stay. Marry me and we'll take that trip to Rome."

"I can't."

He pushed up from the table and she didn't know if he was disappointed or annoyed. Probably both. "Fine then. Do all the thinking you want while I'm gone," Jackson said. "When I get home, we'll settle this." Then he bent to kiss the top of Mia's head. When he straightened up, he looked right at Casey again. "When I get home."

Jackson came home early. He'd rousted his co-pilot out of bed, fired up the jet and set a new personal record for flight speed on the trip back to California. How the hell could he be expected to take care of business in Paris when his head was full of Casey? He'd tried, damn it. He'd wandered the streets of Paris, visited old haunts and never did find the enjoyment he usually experienced when he was wandering the world.

None of it mattered.

Nothing mattered, because he felt like his heart had been scooped out of his chest. She hadn't even answered the damn phone when he'd called. She was avoiding him and he'd had enough. Now it was the middle of the night and he didn't care if she was sound asleep. She was *going* to listen to him. She was *going* to marry him. And they were *going* to be happy, damn it.

He parked his car in the driveway, jumped out and trotted up the narrow walkway to the front door. He stepped inside and the silence hit him like a blow. Taking the stairs two at a time, his own footsteps echoed in the stillness like a heartbeat. He passed his own room, went straight to Casey's and opened the door.

Her bed was empty and the first tendrils of uneasiness began to slip through his system. Turning fast, he crossed to his own room, thinking that maybe she'd come to her senses and had wanted to be in his bed—their bed. But she wasn't there, either.

Across the hall from him was Mia's room and her door stood open. No night-light was burning, though. There were no magical stars shining in the darkness to keep his baby girl company. There was only more silence. He walked across the threshold, and moved through the darkness to the crib, though he knew he'd find it empty. His heart fisted in his chest and the uneasiness quickened into a deeply felt fear like he'd never known before.

Casey had taken Mia and left. He glanced into the baby's closet. Empty. As empty as the house. As empty as his soul.

"Where the hell did they go?" Fear and fury tangled together in the pit of his stomach as he answered his own question. "Dani's."

"Don't tell him anything!"

Jackson looked past a sleepy Mike Sullivan to his wife, standing on the stairs, wearing a pink fluffy robe and a dangerous gleam in her eye. "Dani—"

"Haven't you done enough?" She came down another step and glared at him. "Leave her alone."

Mike moved to block Jackson's view of his wife and planted one hand on the threshold, preventing him entry. "She's not here," he said.

Jackson had been so sure. So positive that Casey would turn to her best friend, he had no idea where to turn now. He looked at the other man and saw sympathy on his face. Jackson responded to it. "Tell me where she is."

Mike shot a glance over his shoulder and winced. Lowering his voice, he looked back at Jackson and said, "I feel for you. I do. But Casey's a friend. And if I want to keep living with my wife…"

"Just tell me if Casey's okay."

"Unhappy, but safe."

Jackson's heart felt like lead in his chest. He didn't want her unhappy. He just wanted *her.* Shoving one hand through his hair, he turned around and looked at the quiet, suburban street. Houses were shut up tight, lights were few. Families were in those houses. Together. And Jackson felt more solitary in that one bleak moment than he ever had before.

"I don't know where to look," he murmured, more to himself than to the man behind him.

Lowering his voice, Mike offered, "You might try talking to your brother."

Whipping his head around, Jackson stared at him. "Which one?"

"Adam."

Turning, Jackson jumped off the porch and ran through the night to the car parked at the curb.

Twelve

"What the *hell* are you doing pounding on my door in the middle of the night?" Adam stood on the threshold, bare-chested, wearing pajama bottoms. His hair was sleep-ruffled and his eyes looked furious.

"Casey's gone." Jackson pushed past his brother, stalked across the foyer straight into Adam's study. "I've got to find her and I don't know where to look." He wasn't used to feeling panicked and he didn't like it. Felt like he was beginning to unravel at the edges and there was nothing he could do about it. "I went to her friend Dani's and her husband told me I should check with you." Facing his older brother, Jackson said, "So? What do you know?"

"I know it's the middle of the night and I'm tired." Adam walked past him to the wet bar, poured himself a brandy and asked, "Do you want one?"

"No, I don't want a damn drink. I want Casey." He shoved both hands through his hair again and gave a good yank. "I'm wasting time just standing here. I should be looking for her. But *where?*"

Adam took a sip of brandy and leaned one elbow on the bar. Studying his brother he asked, "Wherever she is, maybe she doesn't want to be found."

"Too bad," Jackson snapped. He felt as if he were hanging off the edge of the world, the only thing keeping him safe a quickly unraveling rope. "I'm not going to let her leave me. Just walk away like what we have is nothing."

"Uh-huh. Why not?"

"What?" He shot his brother a hard look. "What the hell's that supposed to mean?"

"Simple question. If you don't love her, why do you want her?"

Jackson winced. "Did Casey talk to Gina?"

"You could say that," Adam muttered darkly. "Gina's been talking my ear off about nothing else since. She's not real fond of you at the moment."

Gina wasn't Jackson's problem. Casey was. "I asked her to marry me and she turned me down!" He shouted the words as if he'd been bottling them up for days.

"This surprises you?" Adam snorted a laugh.

Astonished, he said, "Hell yes. She's pregnant with *my* baby. We've already got a daughter. She *should* marry me. It's the only sensible solution."

Adam shook his head, walked across the room and turned on a single standing lamp before sitting down. "God, you really are an idiot."

"Excuse me?"

"Gina's been calling you one for days and I've been defending you, but I can see now, I was wrong."

"How am I the bad guy here?" Jackson asked, defending himself since it was clear as hell nobody else was going to do it. "I wanted to marry her."

"Not because you love her."

"What's love got to do with anything?" Jackson prowled the dark room, shooting the occasional hot glare at his brother, so comfortable in his own house. "Love just complicates things. You get in so deep you don't know which end's up. Who the hell needs that?"

"Everybody," Adam mused, taking a sip of his drink.

Jackson stopped and scrubbed both hands over his face. "I wanted this to be simple. To live with Casey and our daughter. To be together. Happy."

"How's that workin' for you?"

"Not well."

"Tell you anything?"

"Yeah," Jackson said, dropping into the closest chair. "It tells me I'm in deep trouble here. Hell, I've been in deep trouble since the night Casey walked into the hotel bar and smiled at me. I knew it then. I've just been fighting it. Tonight just caps it. I walked into the house and she was gone and I felt like I died. Like there was no air in the world."

"Congratulations," Adam said softly. "You're in love."

"Damn it." Jackson looked at his brother. "I didn't plan on loving her, you know."

"Hell, none of us plans it," Adam said, giving him an

understanding smile. "But you should know…she didn't leave just because of you."

"What else happened?" Jackson took a breath and held it. What else could possibly have gone wrong in a few short days?

"The day after you took the flight to Paris, Marian went to see her at your place."

"Ah, God. What did she do? What did she say?" Jackson jumped to his feet.

"I got all of this from Gina," Adam said on a sigh. "And let me warn you, none of the King women are big fans of yours right now."

"Great."

"Seems Marian tried to buy Casey off. Apparently she offered her a nice little nest egg if she'd leave and agree not to marry you."

"I should have been there. Shouldn't have left. I wanted her to think. To miss me. Backfired big time. I'm the one who missed her." Jackson let out a sigh. "I already know she wouldn't take the money."

Adam scowled at him. "Damn right. According to Gina, Casey told Marian what she could do with her money, said that you and Marian deserved each other and that she wouldn't be a problem anymore."

"We deserve each other? What the hell…why would she—how could—" Jackson had never been more furious. Or more frustrated. Things were happening. Beyond his control. Beyond his ability to fix them. Arrange them into the right kind of order. What the hell was going on with his world?

"You should have called me."

"Casey didn't want us to."

"You're *my* brother."

"And I have to live with *my* wife, who's completely on Casey's side in all this, so no thanks."

Jackson though, hardly heard his older brother. His mind was too busy, racing down several different paths, trying to find the one that would lead him to Casey. Trying to figure out how he could dig himself out of the mess he was now in. She'd taken off, but where would she go? She said she loved the beach, right? So he'd start there. A lot of beach in this country though. This could take awhile.

"I've got to find her. Explain. Talk to her. Maybe the airport in Sacramento. She probably wouldn't want to stay around here and her old house is gone. She's not with Dani, so she's probably headed off somewhere new. Somewhere she thinks I won't be able to find her. Somewhere on the beach."

"That narrows it down."

"Gotta start somewhere."

"Not going to be easy."

Jackson looked at his older brother and smiled grimly. "Nothing about Casey is easy. And you know what? Easy's overrated. I'll find her. You can count on it. And when I do, I'm dragging her back home with me. Where she belongs."

He was halfway across the foyer when Adam's voice stopped him. "Jackson."

"I'll call you from the road, Adam. I'm wasting time here."

"Jackson, stop."

He did. And when he looked over his shoulder at his

brother, Jackson felt the first faint fluttering of hope inside. "You know where she is."

Adam sighed. "If you screw this up, Gina's gonna kill me for telling you."

"*I'll* kill you if you don't."

"I guess we men have got to stick together sometimes," Adam said with a half smile. Then he jerked his thumb at the stairs. "Gina gave Casey your old room on the second floor."

Jackson didn't even pause long enough to thank him. He hit the stairs at a dead run, moving through the darkness on memory alone. He'd grown up in this ranch house. He could find his way blindfolded. And now, knowing that Casey was waiting for him, he knew that nothing could have kept him away.

Outside his old room, he paused, taking a ragged breath and letting it slide from his lungs in an effort to calm himself. But he was as calm as he was going to get, so he turned the knob and slowly opened the door.

Moonlight shone through the windows in slants of silvery light that illuminated the woman asleep on the bed. Her short, blond hair was tousled, the deep red duvet was pushed down to her waist and he smiled when he noticed she was wearing one of his T-shirts to sleep in.

Maybe there was still hope. Maybe she still loved him. Maybe he could bring himself back from the edge he'd blindly walked out on.

Crossing the room with quiet steps, he listened to the sound of her breathing and felt his own smooth out and begin to move in time with hers. She was here. She was safe. And he was in love for the first and last time in his life.

* * *

Casey dreamed of him and in that dream, she caught his scent and inhaled deeply. When he called her name, she turned toward him, even in sleep, reaching for him.

Then he kissed her and the dream was so real, she tasted him, savoring the feel of his lips on hers. So warm, so soft, so… Her eyes flew open and she gasped. "Jackson? How did you—"

He was sitting on the edge of the bed and when he grabbed her before she could scoot back and away, he pulled her across his lap and wrapped both arms around her. She knew she shouldn't lean into him, but she'd missed him so much, pined for him so deeply that the feel of his heartbeat racing in time with her own was too much to resist.

"You scared about ten years off my life tonight," he whispered. "When I got home and you weren't there…"

"I had to leave," she said and remembering why gave her the strength to push out of his arms and scramble back onto the bed. She folded her arms over her chest and held on tight. Just looking at him melted everything inside her. Her heart ached for him. And a voice in her mind whispered, reminding her to be strong. To not settle for less than love.

"I know." Jackson reached out, smoothed her hair, then let his fingertips trail down the side of her face with a touch so light she might have still been dreaming.

He took a breath, looked around the room and asked, "Where's Mia?"

"Sleeping in Emma's room."

"Good," he said. "Good."

"Jackson—"

"No, let me talk first, okay?" He shifted on the bed, getting comfortable, but he didn't reach for her again and Casey wasn't sure what to think about that. "I thought when I left," he said softly, "that you'd miss me so much you'd cave in and marry me. I figured I'd teach you a lesson." He laughed a little, but there was no warmth in the sound. "Turns out, I'm the one who had to learn."

She scooted back, higher against the pillows. Keeping her gaze fixed on Jackson, Casey tried desperately not to let a small bubble of hope become so big that its popping might destroy her.

"I missed you. I missed looking at you, listening to you laugh with Mia. I couldn't *sleep,*" he added with a shake of his head, "because you weren't there to hog the blankets."

"I don't—"

"When I closed my eyes, I saw you. When I walked down the streets in Paris, all I could think was, I wished you were there."

As if he couldn't stand still another minute, he pushed off the bed, walked across his old room to stand beside the window. Moonlight fell on him and Casey couldn't tear her gaze from him.

He turned his head to look at her. "I didn't want to fall in love, Casey. Never planned on it. Never was interested. Love makes life messy. Gives the one you love too much power over you."

She held her breath, waiting, hoping.

"The thing is," he said, "I fell in love anyway. You slipped up on me. You came into my life, knocked it all around, and it shocks the hell out of me to know I like it better that way.

I don't want to go back to my old life, Casey. I want a life with you. With Mia and with our new baby."

Joy rippled through her with such staggering force, Casey thought for a moment she must still be dreaming. Surely it was impossible to be this happy. To have everything she'd ever wanted right in front of her.

Walking back to her side, Jackson sank onto the edge of the bed beside her and looked deeply into her eyes. "Marry me, Casey. This isn't a merger—I'm not trying to build my fortune here. You, Mia and the baby *are* my fortune. The only one I'll ever need."

"Jackson…"

"It isn't convenience, either," he said, talking faster now, wanting to say it all. "This is love, Casey. I can't live my life without you in it. So maybe it's simple after all. I love you. I need you. And if you don't marry me…"

"You'll what?" she asked, already moving toward him, a smile in her eyes.

"I'll…keep asking. I'll tell you I love you every day. Until you're so sick of hearing it you'll marry me just to shut me up."

"I'll never get sick of hearing it," she assured him, sliding onto his lap, wrapping her arms around his neck, trailing her fingers through his thick, soft hair. "Say it again."

"I love you."

"Again."

He buried his face in the curve of her neck. "I love you."

"I love you too, Jackson. So very much."

He held her fiercely, squeezing her until she lost her breath and didn't care if she caught it again.

"So is that a yes?" he demanded.

"It's a yes, Jackson." She grinned at him, her heart whole, her soul singing. Everything was just as it should be. She was in Jackson's arms and the future looked bright. "Of course it's a yes. I love you."

"Thank God," he whispered and held her even tighter.

"Welcome home, Jackson," Casey said, losing herself in the magic of love.

Epilogue

Eight months later...

They named her Molly.

She looked just like her big sister. Just like her cousins.

And her mommy and daddy couldn't have been happier.

Jackson leaned down, kissed Casey and released a breath he felt as though he'd been holding for months. "You're amazing," he said, smiling down at the woman who had made his life absolutely complete.

"As long as you keep believing that, honey," she said, cupping his cheek in the palm of her hand, "everything's going to be great."

"After seeing what you did in here today, I'm convinced," he said. He looked tired, but then, they'd been in labor and delivery for the last nine hours. He'd never left her side and Casey couldn't believe how much easier everything had been because she'd had the man she loved with her through it all.

The King brothers and their wives had already been by, cooing over Molly, promising to keep Mia happy until her parents came home. And now, it was just Casey and Jackson. Molly was asleep in the hospital nursery and the glow of having accomplished another miracle was riding high in Casey's heart.

"I love you," Jackson said, amazement still shining in his eyes as he pulled a small, blue velvet jeweler's box from his pocket.

Casey eyed it warily and even managed a smile. "The last time I saw a box like that, it caused all kinds of trouble."

"I don't know what you're talking about, gorgeous," he said with a grin just before he bent down and dropped a kiss on her mouth. "I'm a married man, desperately in love with my wife."

"Well, in that case…" She took the small box from him, flipped the lid open and gasped. A huge, square-cut sapphire glittered on silk and from either side of the deep blue stone two diamonds winked at her. "Oh, Jackson!"

He took the ring from the box, pushed it onto her right-hand ring finger and said softly, "The sapphire is because it reminded me of your eyes. The twin diamonds are for our girls. The gold ring…that's eternity. With you. Thank you, Casey. For finding me. For loving me."

She lifted her face for his kiss and felt, as she did every day of her life, that her dreams had finally come true.

* * * * *

*Maureen Child will be back with more
Kings of California soon. In the meantime,
don't miss her next exciting Desire,
HIGH-SOCIETY SECRET PREGNANCY,
book one of the
PARK AVENUE SCANDALS series.
It all starts this July…only from Silhouette Desire.*

THOROUGHBRED LEGACY
*The stakes are high when it comes to love,
horse racing, family secrets
and broken promises.*

*A new exciting Harlequin continuity series
coming soon!
Led by* New York Times *bestselling author
Elizabeth Bevarly
FLIRTING WITH TROUBLE*

Here's a preview!

THE DOOR CLOSED behind them, throwing them into darkness and leaving them utterly alone. And the next thing Daniel knew, he heard himself saying, "Marnie, I'm sorry about the way things turned out in Del Mar."

She said nothing at first, only strode across the room and stared out the window beside him. Although he couldn't see her well in the darkness—he still hadn't switched on a light…but then, neither had she—he imagined her expression was a little preoccupied, a little anxious, a little confused.

Finally, very softly, she said, "Are you?"

He nodded, then, worried she wouldn't be able to see the gesture, added, "Yeah. I am. I should have said goodbye to you."

"Yes, you should have."

Actually, he thought, there were a lot of things he should

have done in Del Mar. He'd had *a lot* riding on the Pacific Classic, and even more on his entry, Little Joe, but after meeting Marnie, the Pacific Classic had been the last thing on Daniel's mind. His loss at Del Mar had pretty much ended his career before it had even begun, and he'd had to start all over again, rebuilding from nothing.

He simply had not then and did not now have room in his life for a woman as potent as Marnie Roberts. He was a horseman first and foremost. From the time he was a schoolboy, he'd known what he wanted to do with his life—be the best possible trainer he could be.

He had to make sure Marnie understood—and he understood, too—why things had ended the way they had eight years ago. He just wished he could find the words to do that. Hell, he wished he could find the *thoughts* to do that.

"You made me forget things, Marnie, things that I really needed to remember. And that scared the hell out of me. Little Joe should have won the Classic. He was by far the best horse entered in that race. But I didn't give him the attention he needed and deserved that week, because all I could think about was you. Hell, when I woke up that morning all I wanted to do was lie there and look at you, and then wake you up and make love to you again. If I hadn't left when I did—the way I did—I might still be lying there in that bed with you, thinking about nothing else."

"And would that be so terrible?" she asked.

"Of course not," he told her. "But that wasn't why I was in Del Mar," he repeated. "I was in Del Mar to win a race. That was my job. And my work was the most important thing to me."

She said nothing for a moment, only studied his face in the darkness as if looking for the answer to a very important question. Finally she asked, "And what's the most important thing to you now, Daniel?"

Wasn't the answer to that obvious? "My work," he answered automatically.

She nodded slowly. "Of course," she said softly. "That is, after all, what you do best."

Her comment, too, puzzled him. She made it sound as if being good at what he did was a bad thing.

She bit her lip thoughtfully, her eyes fixed on his, glimmering in the scant moonlight that was filtering through the window. And damned if Daniel didn't find himself wanting to pull her into his arms and kiss her. But as much as it might have felt as if no time had passed since Del Mar, there were eight years between now and then. And eight years was a long time in the best of circumstances. For Daniel and Marnie, it was virtually a lifetime.

So Daniel turned and started for the door, then halted. He couldn't just walk away and leave things as they were, unsettled. He'd done that eight years ago and regretted it.

"It *was* good to see you again, Marnie," he said softly. And since he was being honest, he added, "I hope we see each other again."

She didn't say anything in response, only stood silhouetted against the window with her arms wrapped around her in a way that made him wonder whether she was doing it because she was cold, or if she just needed something—

someone—to hold on to. In either case, Daniel understood.
There was an emptiness clinging to him that he suspected
would be there for a long time.

* * * * *

THOROUGHBRED LEGACY
coming soon wherever books are sold!

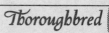 

Cole's Red-Hot Pursuit

Cole Westmoreland is a man who gets what he
wants. And he wants independent and sultry
Patrina Forman! She resists him—until a Montana
blizzard traps them together. For three delicious
nights, Cole indulges Patrina with his brand of
seduction. When the sun comes out, Cole and
Patrina are left to wonder—will this be the end of
the passion that storms between them?

Look for

COLE'S RED-HOT PURSUIT

by USA TODAY bestselling author

BRENDA JACKSON

Available in June 2008 wherever you buy books.

Always Powerful, Passionate and Provocative.

Silhouette®

Romantic
SUSPENSE

Sparked by Danger,
Fueled by Passion.

Seduction Summer:
Seduction in the sand…and a killer on the beach.

Silhouette Romantic Suspense invites you to the hottest
summer yet with three connected stories from some
of our steamiest storytellers! Get ready for…

Killer Temptation
by **Nina Bruhns;**
a millionaire this tempting is worth a little danger.

Killer Passion
by **Sheri WhiteFeather;**
an FBI profiler's forbidden passion incites a
killer's rage,

and

Killer Affair
by **Cindy Dees;**
this affair with a mystery man is to die for.

Look for

KILLER TEMPTATION by Nina Bruhns in June 2008
KILLER PASSION by Sheri WhiteFeather in July 2008
and
KILLER AFFAIR by Cindy Dees in August 2008.

Available wherever you buy books!

Visit Silhouette Books at www.eHarlequin.com

SRS27586

REQUEST YOUR FREE BOOKS!

2 FREE NOVELS PLUS 2 FREE GIFTS!

Silhouette® Desire®

Passionate, Powerful, Provocative!

HARLEQUIN *Presents*

EXTRA

TALL, DARK AND SEXY
The men who never fail—seduction included!

Brooding, successful and arrogant, these men can sweep any female they desire off her feet. But now there's only one woman they want— and they'll use their wealth, power, charm and irresistibly seductive ways to claim her!

Don't miss any of the titles in this exciting collection available June 10, 2008:

#9 THE BILLIONAIRE'S VIRGIN BRIDE
by HELEN BROOKS

#10 HIS MISTRESS BY MARRIAGE
by LEE WILKINSON

#11 THE BRITISH BILLIONAIRE AFFAIR
by SUSANNE JAMES

#12 THE MILLIONAIRE'S MARRIAGE REVENGE
by AMANDA BROWNING

Harlequin Presents EXTRA delivers a themed collection every month featuring 4 new titles.

HPE0608

Royal Seductions

Michelle Celmer delivers a powerful miniseries in
Royal Seductions, where two brothers fight for the
crown and discover love. In *The King's Convenient Bride*,
the king discovers his marriage of convenience to the
woman he's been promised to wed is turning all too
real. The playboy prince proposes a mock engagement
to defuse rumors circulating about him and restore
order to the kingdom…until his pretend fiancée
becomes pregnant in *The Illegitimate Prince's Baby*.

Look for

THE KING'S CONVENIENT BRIDE
&
THE ILLEGITIMATE PRINCE'S BABY

BY MICHELLE CELMER

Available in June 2008 wherever you buy books.

Always Powerful, Passionate and Provocative.

COMING NEXT MONTH

#1873 JEALOUSY & A JEWELLED PROPOSITION—
Yvonne Lindsay
Diamonds Down Under
Determined to avenge his family's name, this billionaire sets out
to take over his biggest competition...and realizes his ex may be
the perfect weapon for revenge.

#1874 COLE'S RED-HOT PURSUIT—Brenda Jackson
After a night of passion, a wealthy sheriff will stop at nothing to
get the woman back into his bed. And he always gets what he wants.

#1875 SEDUCED BY THE ENEMY—Sara Orwig
Platinum Grooms
He has a score to settle with his biggest business rival. Seducing
his enemy's daughter proves to be the perfect way to have his
revenge.

#1876 THE KING'S CONVENIENT BRIDE—
Michelle Celmer
Royal Seductions
An arranged marriage turns all too real when the king falls for his
convenient wife. Don't miss the second book in the series, also
available this June!

#1877 THE ILLEGITIMATE PRINCE'S BABY—
Michelle Celmer
Royal Seductions
The playboy prince proposes a mock engagement...until his
pretend fiancée becomes pregnant! Don't miss the first book in
this series, also on sale this June!

#1878 RICH MAN'S FAKE FIANCÉE—Catherine Mann
The Landis Brothers
Caught in a web of tabloid lies, their only recourse is a fake
engagement. But the passion they feel for one another is all
too real.